Cabin Mate

A Sweet Fake Dating RomCom

Leah Brunner

Leah Brunner Publishing

Contents

To my children. Thank you for dealing with me, amid moving across the country, while I wrote this book. And to the creator of *Minecraft*. You're the real hero. Without your game entertaining my kids, I couldn't have written Brooks' and Molly's lovely story.

Thank you.

Brooks

Freshman Orientation MIT

Walking across the MIT campus, I can barely contain the grin on my face. Year after year, I've watched all three of my older siblings go off to college and pave their way to success. And now it's finally my turn.

I'll get to prove my intelligence, while also enjoying some independence—my mother's love can feel smothering sometimes.

My siblings warned me my first day would be nerve-racking. I huff out a laugh at the thought. I can't remember a time I've ever felt nervous.

A tall, blonde girl walking in the opposite direction must've heard me laugh and stops in her tracks. If her scowl is any indication, she clearly thinks my laughter was directed at her.

"Sorry, I didn't see you there," I tell her, hoping to smooth things over.

The girl opens her mouth to say something, but closes it again as she takes me in, shamelessly looking me up and down. She bites her bottom lip, her expression changing from a scowl to appreciation... She likes what she sees.

Unfortunately, tall blondes aren't my thing. Probably because they remind me too much of my sister.

"Don't worry about it," she says, taking a few steps towards me from the opposite side of the path. A coy smile plays on her lips. "You look like you know your way around campus. Any idea where I can find the software engineering building?"

This happens to me a lot. People mistake my confidence for being older and more knowledgeable than I really am. Or sometimes I'm approached, usually by women, just because I'm the best-looking guy in the room.

Did I ever ask for all the attention? No.

Do I take advantage of it? Absolutely.

I can't help it I hit the genetic jackpot.

I give the girl a friendly smile and a one-shoulder shrug. "Sorry, this is my first day. Heading to freshman orientation."

Her eyebrows raise just enough to confirm she's likely a senior and thought I was too. She never needed directions.

She tucks a strand of hair behind her ear. "Oh, sorry! Have a great first day."

I continue walking, not bothering to look over my shoulder at her. If only my older brothers could see me now ... It's only the first day of school and chicks are already pursuing me.

I'm not in Kansas anymore, though (no Wizard of Oz puns intended). I'm sure college will be different. Maybe a *few* less girls will throw themselves at me than usual. Which is fine by me. I have school to focus on, even though school has always come easily to me as well. After all, I got into MIT because on top of being a handsome trust fund kid ... I'm also brilliant.

Like I said: genetic jackpot.

When the orientation building comes into view, I admire the modern, sleek design. The MIT campus is only a few miles from Harvard, and the contrast between the two is almost comical. Harvard with its classical New England charm, and MIT with its modern, minimalistic, white structures; it's like traveling through time when you drive down Massachusetts Avenue.

Fifteen minutes after leaving my dorm, I arrive at the building my orientation is in—thanks to the handy map I received when I moved in. Once inside, I see the lecture hall is set up in the traditional concert-style setting, with rows of seating starting at the doors and stairs leading downward to more rows. The orientation director, I'm guessing she's around fifty based on her cardigan and slightly grey hair, stands at the bottom of the room in front of a large dry erase board. Unlike most lecture halls, this room isn't dark. Instead, it is clean and white, with large windows lining one side. The natural light feels vibrant and energizing.

Most of the students are already here, with a few more trickling in. Glancing down at my watch, I smirk to myself. I'm one minute early. Just enough to look like a good student, but without seeming desperate to impress the professor like the rest of these early birds.

Looking around, I see an empty seat next to a dark-haired girl. All I can see is the back of her head, but her thick hair hangs down her back in loose curls and there's a scarf tied around her head like a headband. The scarf has a sparrow pattern all over it.

I walk toward her and clear my throat. "Is this seat taken?"

Her head swivels and she glances up at me with the biggest blue eyes I've ever seen. Not the same bright blue as mine and my siblings', but darker and more enchanting. Her cheeks and lips are pink and they stand out against her pale skin.

Her white sweater has delicate pearl buttons, and she's paired it with a silky black skirt that probably goes to her calves, but it's hard to tell when she's seated. She has that coastal grandma vibe that screams old money. There's nothing about her that would make the average person realize she comes from money except for the tasteful diamond stud earrings in her ears. But wealth recognizes wealth.

She's like Massachusetts Avenue: a mixture of old and new. Modern and antique. And she's pretty. Really pretty.

Her smile is genuinely kind as she says, "Nope! Go ahead and sit down."

I take a seat and hold my hand out to shake hers. "Brooks Windell."

She takes my hand. Hers is soft, and her nails are freshly manicured with pale pink polish. Her thumbs have little birds on them, just like the scarf in her hair.

"I'm Molly Vanderbilt," she says. Her voice is like a songbird ... happy and soothing.

Molly. That's not what I was expecting. I hold her gaze for a moment, something wordless running between us like an invisible current.

"Only one name?" I ask before I can stop myself.

"What do you mean?" Her voice is serious, but there's a twinkle in her eyes. I'm not sure if she's amused or irritated.

I smile my flirtatious smile, the one that gets me girls' phone numbers. "You strike me as someone who has at least two names."

It's an old money thing. For some reason, wealthy people can't choose just one name for their daughters.

She huffs out a laugh and lowers her voice to a whisper, leaning in slightly so I can smell her perfume. Chanel No. 5, if I'm not mistaken. My mom used to buy it for my sister, Sophie. Sophie always gave it to a friend because she didn't think the scent suited her ... but it suits Molly.

"I don't know how you guessed that. My full name is Mary Elizabeth. But I go by Molly."

I try not to look smug, but it's hard not to. "It's nice to meet you, Molly."

I'm about to say more, maybe ask for the number of this beautiful girl with the old soul ... but the guy next to her finally notices me and leans forward. He eyes me warily, sizing me up, before draping an arm possessively around Molly.

"Hey, I'm Todd. Molly's boyfriend." His hair and eyes are dark brown, and he's dressed in skinny trousers and a crimson red Harvard sweatshirt over the top of a white dress shirt.

Does he even go to MIT?

I nod my head towards him in a friendly manner. "I'm Brooks," I say simply, not bothering to extend my hand, what with the hostile look he's giving me. But I can't help but ask the question on my mind, "Do you go to MIT or Harvard?" I glance down at his sweatshirt.

He sets his shoulders proudly and smirks. "Harvard. But I came to orientation with my girl for moral support."

She smiles stiffly, making me wonder if she actually wanted him to come to orientation with her. Briefly, I think about asking for her number, anyway. This Todd guy is honestly no competition for me.

But in the end, I decide not to make enemies on the very first day of college. There are plenty of other girls here, anyway.

I just have to wait for another one to fall at my feet.

Chapter 1

Molly

Walking toward the front door of my boyfriend's house—okay, more like a suburban mansion—I stop in my tracks, noticing a hot pink sticky note stuck on the windshield of his sleek black sports car. No, I don't know what type of car it is. Which greatly annoys him.

Normally, his precious baby is in the garage tucked in tight … but today is Friday, which is when his detailer comes and polishes the shiny black coupe until Todd can see his handsome reflection in it.

"No wonder he wanted me to drive tonight," I mutter under my breath as I walk toward the car.

I'm curious what the sticky note is for. Especially since I know how annoyed he'll be to see a sticky note plastered on his freshly detailed baby.

When I'm a few feet away, I see the red lipstick kiss under the handwritten note and my heart stops inside my chest. My mind whirls back to a comment from my best friend Brooks a few months ago ... *I saw Todd having lunch with someone today... a woman. Does he have a sister?*

No. He does not have a sister. I had brushed off his comment, thinking it was probably another man with dark hair and Brooks was mistaken. No biggie. But that red lipstick kiss was, most assuredly, not left by me.

Although, I do love a classic red lip.

Leaning over the hood of the car, I read the loopy feminine writing on the note:

Todd, I had SO much fun with you last night! Call me. -Trudy

My body feels stuck, paralyzed. My stomach flips, and not in a good way. Instead, it's the churning feeling that comes from betrayal. My mind is in such a fog of hurt, I can't think straight.

If someone saw me right now, they'd probably think I'd been turned to stone ... or maybe that I was certifiably insane.

A logical person might stay calm and give their boyfriend of seven years the benefit of the doubt.

I mean, maybe she has the wrong Todd? Or maybe this is a joke from his work buddies? But I have to admit he's been acting off lately ... canceling our plans, and getting that far-off look in his eyes, like he's daydreaming. Probably about someone who isn't me.

Add that to the comment from Brooks, and the truth seems pretty obvious.

And seriously, *Trudy*?? Todd and Trudy. How perfect. Ugh.

I turn and stomp my way up Todd's massive stairway leading to his front door. When I knock, I realize how much of an idiot I've been. We've been together for SEVEN years, and I have to knock ... because he's never given me a key.

Never proposed to me.

Never given me a solid sign of commitment.

The sudden clarity of it all makes my knock turn into more of a belligerent banging. I glance to my left and see one of Todd's hoity-toity neighbors staring at me. He's wearing an expensive tailored suit and a watch that looks just like my father's (meaning it's ridiculously expensive).

I give him a tight smile and do my best *Princess Diaries* wave—just the way my mother taught me. He sniffs, then walks inside his house that looks exactly like Todd's. Every house in this gated community looks the same ... brick that's been painted white, black decorative railings and window panes, and five boxwood trees on either side of the driveway. If it weren't for the house numbers, no one would know which house was their own.

It's always been hard for me to take this neighborhood seriously since Todd works remotely for his father and uncle's billion-dollar media conglomerate. He's likely highly overpaid for the work he does. Daddy's money is definitely footing the bill for this place. My house might not be in a luxurious, gated community ... but I paid for it myself.

A scene pops into my head of two baby birds. They're in their nest, comfortable and safe, until the mama bird tries pushing them to fly. One takes off instantly, soaring and ready to be free. The other refuses to leave, instead opening its mouth and begging for the mama bird to feed him. That's me and Todd.

After several minutes of waiting for an answer, I'm about to turn and leave, but the door finally opens. Two women answer the door and that churning in my stomach returns.

"Hi?" A blonde with a classy bob answers. She's wearing a black cocktail dress that is a little too sexy for my liking. "Can we help you?"

The other has long, dark hair. Her shoulder rests against the door frame. She's also wearing a cocktail dress. It's short, barely reaching the middle of her thighs. Both women are gorgeous.

I can hear laughing from the inside of the house, and try to peek past them, but they scoot closer together like I'm unwelcome.

"Are you here for the music and poetry night?" The one with dark hair asks, assessing me with a judgemental gaze.

Music and poetry night? Did he seriously host a party when he was supposed to take me on a date? And then didn't even invite me?

He couldn't even care enough to *think* about me.

I square my shoulders and plaster the best smile I can muster on my face. "Could I speak with Todd?"

The blonde uses her thumb to gesture toward the backyard. "He's on the back deck getting the stage set up. The gate should be unlocked." She pauses a moment, then shuts the door in my face.

The churning in my stomach is now replaced with hot, unadulterated anger. Partially at Todd, and partially with myself. How have I been so freaking blind?

Eyeing the cobblestone path that leads to the backyard, I contemplate removing my stilettos despite the freezing December weather. But knowing how unpredictable the weather is in Kansas, I'm just thankful it's not covered with ice or snow.

Much to my mother's dismay, I've never been a graceful swan like my older sister. All my lessons and training just couldn't undo my body's natural distaste of gravity. I fake it pretty well ... but don't want to risk twisting my ankle. I take my Christian Louboutin's off to traipse down the stone path barefoot.

The stones are cold on my feet and I pull the collar of my coat up to cover my neck with my free hand. Letting myself in the back gate, I brace myself for what I'm about to see.

Sure enough, not only did Todd get a legitimate stage for tonight, but he and his groupies hung romantic lights and created the perfect ambiance for a poetry reading.

Has he ever put this much effort into planning something for me? Not once.

Todd, along with several other men in nice suits, are putting the final touches on the stage and setting up chairs. I stand there awkwardly, holding my heels in one hand, because what else do I even do? I hadn't thought this far ahead. Before I can decide, the rest of the party comes outside, and now there's a whole crowd of classy party-goers.

Do I confront him in front of all these people? Do I feign ignorance and join the poetry reading?

Realizing I have no interest in joining them, *or* having a public breakup, I clear my throat and hope he hears it over the noise.

To my relief, it works, and his eyes flick up to meet mine. A brief moment of shock passes over his dark eyes before he schools his features into the familiar half-smile I've always loved. But, perhaps, I get the half-smile ... while what's-her-name gets the full one?

He stands and strides toward me, his long legs eating up the space between us quickly. He's wearing a tailored suit that shows off his lean physique. Todd's expression is completely calm, like he doesn't have a care in the world.

For seven years, I've never once worried about Todd cheating. I mean ... he's a decent-looking guy and all, but he sits at a desk all day. So he's always been pretty skinny. He's not the usual type women throw themselves at.

He doesn't even have any chest hair.

Also, he's moody. My father is so stoic, I found Todd's moodiness endearing. I loved that he'd cry while studying a beautiful art piece, and express what he was feeling. Most men only seem to have one emotion, but Todd has enough emotions for fifty of them.

Suddenly he just looks like an overgrown man-child to me. That rush of attraction was ruined the moment I found that note on his car.

"Molls!" he says as he reaches me.

The nickname grates on my nerves even more than usual. Molly is already a shortened version of my full name. Why shorten it even more?

"Heath and I are hosting a little poetry and music night. Do you want to join us? We just threw it together at the last minute, or I would've called you." His voice sounds deep and confident, like always. But the hesitant look in his dark eyes tells me he realizes he's messed up big time.

Glancing around the extravagantly decorated patio, it's obvious this was no last-minute thing. Heath sees me and gives me a two-finger salute. He has light brown hair, muddy brown eyes, and is shorter than the other men here. He's always dressed well, but he doesn't stand out from a crowd ... he's just there.

I nod my head in his direction, unable to bring myself to smile or wave. Heath owns a local art gallery, and he's just as pretentious as Todd. Todd visited the gallery one day and the two hit it off instantly.

I thought Heath was Todd's only friend here in Kansas. But apparently I was wrong.

"Can we talk?" I ask, having to raise my voice slightly to be heard over the chatter and laughter. "Now."

The party-goers pause briefly to stare at me before going back to ignoring my presence.

Todd ignores my demand and looks me up and down with a flirtatious look. "You look gorgeous. Where are you headed?" He has the audacity to wink at me and then leans in like he's going to kiss me.

I dodge his kiss and put my palm right in front of his face. "Just stop."

"Aw, come on. It's just a small get-together. Don't get jealous."

Closing my eyes, I count to three before responding. "What about our date?"

He scratches the top of his head, looking confused for a moment. Finally, realization hits him, and he blows out a deep breath. "Crap. Was that tonight?" Todd runs a hand through his perfectly combed hair. "Maybe Heath can handle the party."

"Don't bother, Todd." I sigh. "I can't do this anymore."

He brings a hand up and rests it on my shoulder. "You're overreacting. Let's just reschedule for tomorrow night?"

I scoff. "Let's reschedule for … never. Just call up Trish if you get lonely and need a date."

I turn to leave, and he grabs my elbow. "Trish?" His jaw clenches as he says her name.

"Yeah, the woman who had so much fun with you last night. She left the sweetest little note on your car."

He laughs. "I don't know anyone named Trish. Maybe it was from Trudy?" His eyes go wide, realizing his mistake. "I mean—I don't know a Trudy either!"

Grabbing my elbow back from his hand, I set my shoulders once again and walk out of his yard with all the dignity I have left.

Unsurprisingly, Todd doesn't bother coming after me.

Chapter 2

Brooks

Molly shows up at my door, looking murderous. It's a cold December evening, and she's wearing a cream-colored wool trench coat with intricate gold buttons.

"Can I come in?" she asks, not giving me a chance to respond before brushing past me.

"Of course," I answer, even though she's already removed her designer shoes—which are now unceremoniously tossed onto the white marble floor of the entryway.

I close the door behind us and cross my arms over my chest. "What's wrong?"

Molly removes her coat and actually takes the time to hang it on a peg, her tiny five-foot-four frame having to stand on her tiptoes to reach it. She plows past me again, straight toward the kitchen without sparing me another glance.

I look after her, still wondering why she's upset. She looks gorgeous ... she always does. But her face is smudged with mascara and her hair is mussed like she tried to yank it all out. She's like a really cute raccoon with designer shoes.

"Do you have ice cream?" she asks, sparing a glance at me over her shoulder.

"Yep," I answer, following her into the large chef's kitchen ... a kitchen that's wasted on me since it's only used to store take-out. "Mint chocolate chip," I add, because that's her favorite flavor, and I always keep some on hand.

She doesn't smile, but walks straight to the freezer, pulls out the carton, then moves toward the drawer that holds the silverware. She stares into the drawer for a second, before changing her mind and opening the drawer next to it instead. Molly selects a large wooden spoon and heads into the living room.

I chase after her and reach her just as she pulls a big fluffy blanket off the couch and wraps herself up in it before sitting down, still holding the ice cream to her chest.

The look of anger in her face is gone now, replaced with the shine of tears. All I want to do is pull her into my arms and wipe her tears away.

Molly opens the ice cream and hands me the lid without so much as looking at me. Then she dips her spoon in and starts devouring it, still managing to look pretty somehow with her round eyes, perfect lips—pouty on the bottom, cupid's bow on top—shiny, dark hair twisted up into a sleek updo, and wearing a dress even my particular mother would be jealous of.

It irks me not knowing how to help. All I can do is wait for her to speak.

I hate when she's upset … but there's something nice about knowing I'm the only one she feels comfortable letting her hair down with—figuratively speaking, of course. Molly's hair is always perfectly styled. No crunches in sight, or whatever those things from the eighties are called. That loser Todd probably hasn't even seen her like this. He's the kind of self-entitled prick who'd want his girlfriend to stay prim and proper all the time. And he's so scrawny, there's no way he keeps his freezer stocked with emotional support ice cream. Honestly, some ice cream might help him bulk up a bit.

I wait until she reaches the bottom of the ice cream container—and not one of those measly little pints, but a half gallon one—before asking her again what's wrong. With a heavy sigh she begins, her voice still a little shaky.

"Todd was supposed to take me out tonight. So I went to his house—"

I hold my hand up to stop her. Already feeling irate. "He couldn't even pick you up for your date?" My voice comes out louder than I wanted it to.

"Would you just let me finish?"

Forcing myself to relax, I fold my hands together and close my eyes for a second. "Sorry. Continue."

Molly rolls her eyes. "Anyway, I didn't even make it to his front door, before I saw a note from another woman on his car. Signed with a lipstick kiss."

One of my eyebrows raises slightly, the kind of eyebrow action that silently says *I'm going to murder him*. Realizing what my face is doing, I relax my expression real quick. But she looks concerned, so she definitely noticed the eyebrow.

Her shoulders relax slightly when my eyebrow calms down, and she continues her story. "And he also forgot about our date, and was setting up a poetry night for his friends."

Despite the burning rage I feel, I work my very hardest to nod sympathetically and just listen to her.

"So, I broke up with him."

She stares at me, waiting for my response. My left eye twitches with barely suppressed rage. When I saw him a few months ago at dinner with a blonde, I was hoping it was purely innocent. I've never liked the guy, but for Molly's sake, I hoped he wasn't capable of being *this* vile of a human.

Molly and Todd have broken up several times over the years. Normally, it's over forgotten dates, or Todd ignoring her because he's having a bad day. A few times he's completely missed her birthday. They stay broken up for a few days, and then things will be good with them for a few months. He'll be attentive and sweet, romantic even. Once he's sure she's going to stick around, he slips and goes back to his same old ways.

How someone could have a brilliant woman like Molly and not worship the ground she walks on is a mystery to me. And every time he hurts her, I have to refrain myself from bashing his face in. Right now, all I want to do is go over to Todd's, interrupt his "poetry night," and give him a bloody lip. But that'll just get me thrown in prison, and I'm way too pretty to go to prison.

And *why* does she keep giving him chances? Here's this amazing woman who's insanely smart and a total knock-out, but she can't see it for herself. She deserves so much better than Todd. And she should *never* settle for less than she deserves.

Have I tried convincing her not to take him back? That he's all wrong for her? Of course.

But she and Todd have known each other since child-hood. Their mothers are best friends ... and I know her mom puts a lot of pressure on her to be with him. Why she'd *want* her to stay with such a tool is beyond my comprehension.

Molly blows her nose rather ungracefully, interrupting my thoughts and dragging me back into the present. "I know what you're thinking," she says. "And I'm not letting you go over there and beat him up. You're not cut out for prison."

This is the scary thing about having a best friend. They can read your thoughts and sense your emotions. I'd had friends before Molly came into the picture ... but no one could read me the way Molly can. It's like there's this invisible thread between us, linking us together. I've never felt this pull to anyone else ... ever.

"Okay." I say through gritted teeth. Closing my eyes, I inhale a long, deep breath and blow it out slowly. Then I sit next to her on the couch, leaning forward and resting my elbows on my knees. "I'm so sorry he hurt you, Molly. What can I do?"

"Call my mother and tell her to stop wasting her breath trying to convince me to give Todd another chance?" She says with a groan, dropping her head back against the couch and looking up at the ceiling. "She can just get over her ridiculous dream of me and her best friend's son getting married."

"You know I will, just give me her number." I rest my arm on the couch behind her. I'd give anything to wrap my arm around her and pull her into me ... but this isn't the time. The feel of her body against mine would definitely make me feel *too* friendly toward my best friend. That pesky eyebrow wants to go rogue and shoot up again, but I smooth it with the back of my hand.

She lifts her head and turns her blue-eyed gaze on me, the force of it making my heart speed up. "I know you would." She brings one hand up to pat my shoulder. "Hopefully, my mother *and* Todd will leave me alone. Oh! And maybe he'll move back to Massachusetts where he belongs?"

I smile wistfully to myself. Todd moving far away would be my dream come true. "We can only hope."

"Mildred is going to blow a gasket about this ... especially with the wedding coming up in a few weeks."

I grimace, thinking back to our college graduation. Mildred wore a red sequin dress and heels so high they looked like stilts. To me, it seemed like she couldn't handle having the attention on her sister for even one day. Now that she's a bride, I can't even imagine how unbearable she must be.

"She's marrying Todd's cousin, right?" I ask, remembering Molly's sister is marrying a Du Pont.

"Yep. Preston. And Todd is Preston's best man." She angles her face to the side and looks up at me. "Todd and I are supposed to enter the ceremony together, hand in hand."

A growl rumbles quietly in my throat before I can stop it. I'm hoping she didn't hear it.

"Preston is a good guy, though," Molly says, "Don't hold his relation to Todd against him."

"I can't believe your parents even allow you to hang out with me. Seeing as I'm not a Du Pont." I nudge her with my elbow and she smiles for the first time since she walked through my front door.

"Their only beef with you is that you're only a millionaire and not a billionaire. You peasant." She purses her lips, trying to look serious.

I give her a pointed look. "Not a billionaire *yet*."

She laughs, the sound making my smile grow even bigger than it already was. I love how we can roast each other. "Um, I think you're forgetting that I run the business and finance side of your so-called 'prospective billion-dollar company.'" Her hands go up in air quotes and I laugh. "I hate to be the bearer of bad news, but your billionaire status isn't happening anytime soon."

"Alright, little miss negativity," I concede. "But it's *not* impossible."

The following morning, my alarm goes off at seven. Way too early for a Saturday morning. But when my congressman brother, Madden, has time to squeeze me into his hectic schedule, I jump at the chance to hang with him.

I slip on my comfiest jeans. They're distressed and give me that "model off-duty" look. Pairing it with my D.C. Eagles hoodie that Madden got me, my casual look is complete. Never would've pegged my buttoned-up oldest brother as a hockey fan, but Washington D.C. has changed him. Or at least I tell him so, just to annoy him. Being friends with your siblings once you're all adults is pretty cool, but I haven't hung up my annoying little brother hat completely.

Striding from my master bedroom into the living room, I smile to myself when I see the mess of ice cream cartons, popcorn kernels, and hot cocoa mugs scattered about. Evidence of my and Molly's impromptu movie night last night. The mess makes my house look cozier and more lived-in. Despite living here for a few years, I don't have a lot of furniture or pictures on the walls. Actually, the only picture I hung up is a painting Molly gifted me when I bought the house. It's of a large Highland cow, and it hangs front and center above my mantle.

I named him Cowlvin.

Molly stayed later last night than I thought she would. Maybe she just didn't want to be alone. No complaints from me, though; I finally had the chance to introduce her to a classic Christmas movie: *Die Hard*. Since meeting Molly in college, I've introduced her to most of my favorite movies. She made me sit through the six-hour adaptation of *Pride and Prejudice*, so I don't feel too bad.

I wink at Cowlvin before grabbing my truck keys from the coffee table and heading to breakfast.

With one last refreshing inhale of the wonderfully freezing-cold morning air, I open the front door of the quaint brick building that houses one of our favorite breakfast cafes. Everyone keeps their heaters way too high during the winter, so I'll soak up the chill before I inevitably start sweating to death. The overhead bell jingles, and one of the waitresses smiles at me and says good morning. I nod politely before looking around for my brothers.

Immediately, I spot Madden at our usual corner booth. I'd recognize the confident set of his broad shoulders from a mile away. Plus, he's the only person I know who'd be wearing a dress shirt on a Saturday morning. What I wasn't expecting was that it's not our brother-in-law sitting next to him, but Madden's wife, Odette.

I walk over to greet them, smiling at my sister-in-law, who's dressed casually compared to her husband. Her red hair is up in a messy bun and a chunky green sweater swallows up her tiny form.

"Where's Drew?" I ask.

Madden bristles, like there's a bad taste in his mouth. "He texted five minutes ago saying he's busy *newlywed-ding*."

I cringe and Madden shivers dramatically. "Does that mean what I think it means?"

"I didn't inquire. I don't want to know."

"True. I don't want to think about our sister *newlywed-ding*." The made-up verb sounds strange even coming out of my mouth.

Madden winces. "Can we just never repeat that word again?"

Odette shakes her head at our dramatics. "I hope it's okay I interrupted your guy time. Your mom wanted the kids to come over for pancakes this morning. And I needed some adult interaction before Madden heads back to D.C. again."

"Of course! You're way nicer to look at than Drew, anyway." I give her an overly dramatic wink, knowing it will irritate Madden. He glares at me and Odette laughs.

Our usual waitress brings three white mugs to our table and sets them down as I slide into the booth across from Madden and Odette.

"Hey, Sugar!" Bonnie greets me warmly, her eyes crinkling in the corners.

I give her my winning smile. "How's the prettiest girl in the Midwest doing on this glorious morning?"

She pretends to fluff her short, white hair. "Oh, stop! You rascal!" Bonnie giggles, then heads back toward the kitchen.

Madden shakes his head. "You just can't help yourself, can you?"

His words give me pause, and my thoughts trail back to Molly ... about how she's single. About how she's hopefully done with Todd Du Pont—or as I like to call him, Turd Da Punk—for good.

Madden must see something in my facial expression and eyes me with a curious expression. "Okay, what's up?" he asks, setting his coffee mug down and giving me his full attention.

I huff out a laugh. It sounds fake, even to me. "What? Nothing is up."

He continues staring me down. I run a hand through my hair, trying to appear casual, but he keeps staring.

"Listen," Madden says in a serious tone. "Drew is doing ... let's not even go there. And David is gallivanting around the world with Isa." He pauses and I gulp. "If you have something on your mind, now is your chance to discuss whatever it is without an audience."

Madden and I stare at each other for a few seconds before I breathe out a heavy sigh. "Molly is single."

"Again?" Madden asks, his face void of emotion. He then slowly picks up his mug again and takes a drink, his eyes not leaving mine.

Odette glances from me to Madden and then back again. "Can somebody fill me in on what the heck is going on?"

Madden smiles at her sympathetically before shooting me a tentative glance. I can tell he's silently asking my permission to explain things to Odette. I nod once.

"Brooksy here has had it bad for his bestie for, what? Five years now?" Odette's eyes widen and he continues. "She's the only girl to ever friend zone the poor boy."

My sister-in-law glances at me, her eyes big and sad like Madden just told her my dog died or something. "Aw, Brooks."

Madden doesn't feel sorry for me at all and keeps trucking along. "Anyway, she and her idiot boyfriend have broken up at least half a dozen times. And every time, Brooks gets his hopes up that *this* time will be different."

Odette blinks slowly a few times, wrapping her mind around this news. "Wow. That's rough. Working together must be torture. But I mean ... it's not like you haven't stayed *busy* all these years." She's too nice to come right out and call me a dude-bro.

"Yeah, it sucks," I admit.

Madden rests his elbows on the table and clasps his hands together. "So, do you like her because she's a challenge for you? Or do you really think she's *the one?*" he lowers his voice on the last two words to give them more impact. "And if it's the latter, what are you going to do about it?"

Bonnie interrupts, arriving at our table with our orders. She places our plates in front of us, notices our nearly empty mugs, and hustles back to the kitchen for the coffee pot. I relax against the back of the booth and drape my arm across the top, thankful for the reprieve from my brother's probing questions. Bonnie returns and tops us off with a sweet smile and leaves us to our conversation.

Once she's gone, I finally answer: "If soulmates are real, Molly is mine."

"I don't get it," Odette says, looking stupefied. She takes a bite of her scrambled eggs, then chews and swallows it quickly. "Why date so many women when you're in love with Molly?"

"Because she's always been with Todd!" I throw my hands up in frustration. "Do you know how much it sucks to sit home alone when the girl you've fallen for is out on a date with another guy?"

"Sooo, you were distracting yourself?" Her nose scrunches up, causing her freckles to bunch together.

"Yes. Well, kind of. I kept hoping I'd fall for someone else and get over her."

"You *used* other women to try to get over someone else?"

Madden snickers at his wife's intrusive questions and I narrow my eyes at him before shoving an entire slice of bacon in my mouth. "Well, it sounds terrible when you put it like that," I talk out of the side of my mouth. My words are slightly muddled from my mouth being full. My mother would smack me in the head if she saw me.

They're both staring at me with unamused expressions.

I sigh. "I had a rule that I'd never go on a second date with someone unless I genuinely felt something for them."

Madden scoffs. "And after hundreds of women, you felt nothing? Dude."

"Hundreds?? Damn, bro. You hurt me." I bring my hand to my chest like my heart hurts.

He rolls his eyes. "Okay, how many?"

"I didn't keep track. That's weird."

Odette scoots her plate away from her and pins me with her serious green eyes. She makes me feel like I'm under one of those detective lamps in the movies. The ones they use to question criminals. "So, if you really think she's the girl for you, what's the plan then?"

"I can't do anything." I huff out an annoyed sigh and widen my eyes, waiting for him to remember why I can't act on my feelings for Molly. He has an expression on his face like I just gave him the world's most challenging algebra equation. "The bet!"

"Oooh right." He shrugs. "You can't date anyone for four months, right? Wait, you didn't sign anything, did you?" He's using his lawyer voice, and I have to hold back a laugh.

"It's a bet, Madden. Not a prenup." I scoff. "But you and I both know David will make me hold up my end of the bargain."

He nods and his mouth goes up in a grin. "Oh, now I remember. If you break your end of the deal, you have to run naked through Mom's annual garden party at the country club."

"Yes. And as good as I look naked, I really don't want to do that. Some of those old ladies would keel over. And I don't want any blood on my hands." I chug another big gulp of coffee, trying to erase the picture from my mind.

"It's nearly the middle of December already. You can't have that much longer left, right?"

"True," Odette adds. "Your dating ban started months ago!" She looks down at her plate and laughs to herself.

"I still can't believe David went on a hiking excursion ... and then eloped in Venice."

"Right?" I groan. "I never would have agreed to the bet if I thought he'd actually do something spontaneous. I made it way too easy for him to win."

Madden and Odette chuckle, like this is the most entertaining thing ever. They look way too amused, and it's causing my mood to sour. I pick up my buttermilk biscuit and throw it at Madden's face. He quickly dodges it. Damn the Windell athleticism. And what a waste of a perfectly delicious biscuit ... Any southerner would have my hide if they saw that.

"Don't get your panties in a twist," Madden says, eye-ing me in that annoyed older-brother way. "Just wait until your no-dating thing is over, and then ask Molly out." He shrugs.

I frown down at my half-eaten eggs and bacon. "That's an entire month that Todd can convince her to get back together with him."

Deep down, I'm hoping this is the time she will finally be done with him for good. Even if she doesn't want to be with me... which would be crushing... at least she could find someone who treats her right.

Madden looks at me sympathetically for the first time since this conversation started. Maybe he's finally real-izing how serious my feelings for Molly are?

Right when I think he's going to give me some epic big brother wisdom, he reaches across the table and tousles my hair. "This might be the last thing you want to hear... but it would make my entire year if you had to run through the garden party in nothing but your birthday suit."

Odette smacks him on the shoulder but can't suppress her laughter.

Chapter 3

Molly

"**M**olly! Call. Me. Back! I know you're avoiding me. But did you honestly think I wouldn't be upset that my maid of honor broke up with the best man two weeks before the wedding?! Listen, all I'm asking is you get back together with him for two weeks. Then, as soon as the wedding is done, BAM! Break up. Simple as that. Or better yet, marry him! And then we can both be Du Ponts!"*

My sister's shrill, stressed out voice fades away as her voicemail ends. I sink back into my comfy bed and try to go back to sleep. It's barely eight a.m... on a Sunday morning, no less. Why is she even up?

"Thanks a lot, Mildred. I'm wide awake now," I grumble into my pillow.

I briefly consider finally calling her back and getting it over with, but it's too early for that. She's not always this dramatic ... but ever since she got engaged, she's been the ultimate Bridezilla. Last month, she left me a voice-mail sobbing so dramatically I could barely understand her. After listening to the voicemail three times, I finally understood half of what she was saying... something about the china they ordered being the wrong shade of white.

So yeah, melodramatic voicemails from my sister aren't anything new, but they've tripled in the days since I ended things with Todd. My phone history makes it look like I have a stalker, not a sister.

I should've known that Todd, being the *todd*-ler that he is, would throw a tantrum the moment I ended things. Informing our families that I broke up with him "out of nowhere."

Groaning, I grab my phone from my nightstand again, this time noticing my background is still a photo of me and Todd. We're standing in front of an abstract painting that Todd purchased from Heath's gallery. I study the picture, noticing Todd's hand on my waist is limp, like he doesn't want to be touching me. He's also not looking at the camera, but off in the distance somewhere. A feeling of sadness washes over me... Todd and I had some good years together, where he really loved me.

Or was it all in my head?

I tap on my photos and select a recent one of me and Brooks. He's standing behind me in line at the movie theater, giving me moose ears with his large hands. He's grinning the way he always does, his smile so big it takes over his entire face. He's all brightness and joy and laughter. I smile just looking at the picture.

Since I was old enough to notice boys, I've always gone for the dark and broody ones. The serious guys who appreciate the arts... the ones that write you poems... the ones with deep souls. Which is all fine and good until they don't get their way and they take all that emotion out on you.

I roll out of bed to get ready for the day, and my phone rings again. I glance at the screen to see my mother is calling this time. I want to speak with her even less than I do Mildred. She'll simply tell me to suck it up and forgive Todd, like she always does. In her mind, he and Mildred's fiancé, Preston, are the ultimate billionaire bachelors.

Why can't my family be as supportive and understanding as Brooks is? He's the one person who's always in my corner, always on my side. He's been the most supportive person in my life since college... which is probably why Todd always hated him.

Deciding to put it all out of my mind, I turn on a Nat King Cole Christmas album on my Bluetooth speaker and throw on a little makeup since my friends will be here in an hour for coffee. I'm eager to see them and fill them in on the drama that is my life.

An hour later, I barely get the door open before Hope and Layla barrel into me with aggressive hugs. It took me a bit to get used to Midwesterners and how open and honest they are. Even their hugs are ungraceful... but I wouldn't change them. I love how real they are.

Layla pulls back first and looks me up and down, her dark brown eyes surveying me like she's looking for clues. Hope soon joins in the search for... I'm honestly not sure. They glance at each other with a quizzical expression.

"What are you looking for?" I ask, crossing my arms self consciously.

"Are you okay?" Hope responds a little too quickly. Her blonde curls bobbing as she shakes her head, and her green eyes shifting back and forth between me and Layla.

Layla smiles, her eyes filled with sympathy. "We're just worried about you. Your text about meeting for coffee sounded urgent."

My eyebrows draw together slightly, because I'm pretty sure my text said, *hey girls, wanna come over for coffee tomorrow morning?* I even added a heart emoji.

"Did you guys talk to Brooks?"

A knowing look passes between the two of them. It's all very conspiratorial. Finally, they both answer no. I sigh and decide to let it go because I really need a cup of coffee.

"Hmm, okay. Let's get caffeinated already." I walk in the direction of the kitchen.

They follow closely behind me through the foyer and into the spacious kitchen. I purchased this gorgeous Victorian home this summer. It had always been my dream to live in an old home with lots of character. I simply had to wait for the one I wanted to come available. My parents thought I was crazy since it needed a ton of work and modernization, but my contractor made her beautiful in no time leaving just enough of the original features, such as rounded doorways and hardwood floors, so as to not remove all the character of the home. He even built me a new display case for my antique spoon collection. The outside of the house is spectacular as well, painted in various shades of brown and pink. It's like a real-life gingerbread house.

But the crowning glory of the entire house? A long, antique bar that rests along one of my kitchen walls. I use it as my coffee bar. Not only is it a gorgeous piece

of furniture, but it's big enough to house my commer-
cial-sized espresso machine.

I *love* coffee.

Everyone says they love coffee... but coffee is an art
form. True coffee lovers pour their heart and soul into
it.

Taking three large, white mugs from a shelf under the
bar and a few long-handled spoons, I turn toward the
girls and ask them what they'd like.

"Americano for me, please," Layla says, keeping her
order simple as usual.

"Will we ever get to use your fancy spoon collection?
They're too pretty not to be used." Hope eyes the plain,
silver spoons on the coffee bar.

"Absolutely not! My antique spoons are my babies."

"You're such an old lady sometimes," Hope says with
a sigh.

I laugh. "What's your order?"

She perks up. "What's today's special?"

She knows me too well. I adore playing barista for
my friends. "I've been experimenting with an apple pie
spice latte recipe ... It's pretty good."

"Perfect! I'll have that," she says before taking a seat
at the small round table in my breakfast nook.

Layla joins her there, and I begin prepping my espresso machine for our drinks.

"Sooo, what's new with you?" I hear Layla ask from the table. My back is turned toward them, but I catch a hint of humor in her voice.

"I'm not sure how you two figured out I broke up with Todd... but I'll find out, eventually."

Hope gasps. It sounds fake. "Oh, my gosh! I'm so sorry." Her voice is sweet but slightly exaggerated.

I glance at them over my shoulder and narrow my eyes, letting them know I'm onto their weird charade. As I make our drinks, I fill them in on the note I found on Todd's car and then how I confronted him about it. I explain he was hosting a party and forgot about our date. While telling my friends the details, I realize that I'm surprisingly calm about the whole thing. It feels as if Todd and I have been back and forth so many times ... just stagnant ... that our breakup was bound to happen sooner or later.

They both jump up from their seats and pull me into a big group hug.

"Molly, I'm so sorry. Todd is even worse than I thought," Layla says as she pulls back.

Hope nods in agreement. "If I ever see him again, I don't think I'll be able to stop myself from slapping him."

I smile and huff out a laugh. "I definitely won't stop you."

"And a poetry party?" Layla cringes.

Hope crinkles her nose. "Yeah, that sounds like the most boring party ever." She takes a dainty sip of her latte. "He should've asked for Brooks's help planning a party. Now that man knows how to have fun."

I finish our coffees and bring them to the table on a cute wooden tray.

Layla raises her eyebrows appreciatively. Brooks may not be my type, what with his blonde locks and bright personality, but I can see the appeal he has and why women love him. Not only because he's so outgoing and vivacious... but all those muscles. If you're into that sort of thing.

Before Layla and Hope came along, Brooks was the only genuine friend I had. Even when Todd and I were broken up, I had no desire to mess up my friendship with Brooks by getting romantically involved, and I'm positive Brooks feels the same way.

"He's your boss," I waggle my finger in mock reprimand. "Keep it clean."

Hope giggles into her latte.

"So are you!" Layla laughs.

Shrugging, I take a drink of my apple pie spice latte, savoring the sweet but spicy flavor of it.

I clear my throat and change the subject, "So now my sister is freaking out that I ruined her wedding. But I'm not sure what the big deal is. Everyone's eyes will be on Mildred and Preston. No one will even notice if things are awkward between the maid of honor and the best man."

"Well, she may have a point. Didn't Todd make a big scene one summer right after one of your breakups?" Hope cringes at the thought.

Layla rolls her eyes. "Oh yeah. He crashed your vacation in Turks and Caicos, right? Blazing drunk and yelling about how you ruined his life?"

"Well, yeah. But it's his cousin's wedding. All of his family will be there. I don't think he'd pull a stunt like that." I pause, not feeling entirely confident in my own words. But I straighten my shoulders and continue anyway. "I'm sure Todd and I can keep things cordial."

Layla rubs her chin thoughtfully with her thumb and forefinger. "You should find a date though ... That way, Todd will leave you alone."

Hope nods enthusiastically. "Oh yes, bonus points if he thinks you're dating the guy."

I nearly spit out my latte. "In *two* weeks? You seriously think he'd buy that?"

Hope shrugs. "He's highly emotional and also insecure ... so yeah."

"You have a point. He does always seem eager to get back together. Although I'm not sure why, since he seems pretty uninterested in me when we're dating." I tap my index finger on my bottom lip as I think. "Actually, bringing a date might even keep my mother from bothering me about Todd."

Layla and Hope glance at each other over the rims of their mugs. Their eyes are gleaming with whatever scheme they're coming up with.

"What's that look?" My eyes move back and forth from Hope to Layla and back.

They slowly set their cups down and their lips turn up into ornery smiles. "I think we know the perfect man for the job," Layla says, her voice ringing with excitement.

"And Todd already hates him," Hope adds.

Realizing exactly where they're going with this, I firmly say, "No. Absolutely not."

"Oh, come on! He's perfect!" Layla whines, scooting closer to me like proximity will win me over somehow.

"He's wealthy, handsome. You already know you can trust him. Did I mention Todd hates him?" Hope pleads, scooting toward me on the opposite side.

I'm sandwiched between them. Both of their eyes look big and shiny like puppies begging for a treat.

"Isn't there anyone you can think of besides Brooks? Our friendship is so important to me; I don't want him to feel like I'm taking advantage of him."

Layla huffs out a sigh. "Who else are you going to find in *two* weeks?"

Looking down at my now empty mug, I answer, "I don't know … Maybe I can find an escort service? Like in *The Wedding Date*."

"But Brooks would do it for free!" Layla says with a grin.

"Just talk to him. It would all be fake, and he'd be the perfect person to keep Todd from bothering you. It never hurts to ask … He can always say no," Hope says, trying one last time to convince me.

"That's true. He could just say no." Layla nods in agreement.

Admitting defeat, my shoulders slump and I blow out a deep breath. "I guess you're right. I'll ask … but I'm not pressuring him if he's hesitant."

Blindingly large grins emerge on their faces, and I wonder what I'm getting myself into.

That evening, as I'm kneading dough for French bread, my phone starts ringing. My hands are covered in bread dough, and I spin in a circle to see what I can use to clean them off. My butcher block countertops are a mess of ingredients from making bread and home-made Alfredo sauce for dinner. Spotting a tea towel, I grab it and clean my hands off enough to answer my phone.

Mildred is FaceTiming me. I sigh, not wanting to answer. But I've put her off for two days already.

I swipe to answer, and my sister's flawless face and silky blonde hair pops up on my screen. She'd be even prettier if her face wasn't pinched into an annoyed expression. Somewhere between a glare and a sob.

"Hey, sis!" I answer cheerfully, slapping my best smile on my face. "What's up?"

"What's up?!" She demands. "You can't be serious! How could you do this to me?" A tear streams down her face and she dabs at it carefully so as not to mess up her makeup.

Closing my eyes, I count to three before responding. "Mildred, *I'm* the one who got cheated on. I didn't time this breakup just to ruin your special day."

"Cheated on? Todd said you overreacted about a little get-together he had with some friends. He said you completely flew off the handle," she states, crossing her arms over her white cashmere sweater.

I withhold an eye roll. "Let me ask you this: If you found a note from another woman on Preston's car, *and* found out he hosted an entire party without so much as inviting you, what would you have done?"

She scoffs and waves her hand in the air like the scenario isn't a big deal. "Molly ... Preston and Todd are the heirs to a multi-billion-dollar media conglomerate. Marrying men like them is everything women dream of! So, of course, I'd turn a blind eye." She pauses. "But I *am* sorry that happened to you. That sucks."

I blink rapidly, trying to understand what she just said. I knew money was important to Mildred, but not to that extent. "Why would you do that? You have your trust fund to support yourself. You don't even need Preston's money."

"Well, first, Preston would never do that."

I nod. My sister's fiancé is obsessed with her. So she's probably right.

"And second, I'm used to this lifestyle and I'm not about to work and be all independent like you." She huffs out a laugh like the thought is utterly ridiculous.

"I find fulfillment in my work, Mildred," I grit out through clenched teeth, which I'm hoping looks like a smile.

"And thank goodness you do, because it's important work!" She pauses and turns around, as if making sure no one is behind her. "You should see Crystal's botched boob job," she whispers, cupping a hand around her mouth. "Her surgeon definitely didn't use the implants you designed."

I forgot how frustrating it is talking to my sister. As if Brooks and I started our medical engineering company just for the sake of rich women getting good boob jobs.

But it goes way beyond that. It's pointless to tell Mildred this, though. I've tried before.

"Yep. It *is* important work."

Mildred sighs heavily, causing her blown-out curtain bangs to fly up in the air. "Anyway, back to the wedding! You at least have to get a date ..." she trails off and bites her bottom lip.

"Wait, really?" I ask, surprised she's not trying to make me go with Todd. "Um, why do you have that weird look on your face?"

"Okay fine, I'll tell you! You don't have to freak out." She rolls her eyes like I threatened her to get top secret information. "You didn't hear it from me ... but Preston told me that Todd found another woman to bring as his date already ... her name is awful, something like Tina or Tiana."

"Trudy?"

"Oh yes! That's it!" She brings her face closer to the phone. "Anyway, I'm telling you so you can bring a date ... which will make him jealous ... which will make him finally propose."

My eyes widen slightly at the fact that he's bringing the woman he cheated on me with. Maybe Hope and Layla were right and he actually *will* make a scene at the wedding. Or perhaps he's hoping *I'll* be the one to make a scene.

I huff out an annoyed laugh. "I don't want him to propose." I genuinely don't want to marry a man like Todd. And it sucks that it took me seven years to see that.

"You're heartbroken. You don't know what you want," she states, completely writing off my comment. "I have to go. Preston just got here to go over the seating assignments for the reception! And don't forget to get a date. Or you're dead to me!" She yells the last part at the screen before hanging up so fast I can't get another word in.

I set my phone down on the countertop with an exaggerated groan.

Would Brooks actually agree to be my date? We've been friends for so long, surely it wouldn't make things weird between us. Brooks has seen me on my best and worst days and nothing has ever altered our friendship. So maybe this ruse could just be a fun little inside joke we talk about for years to come?

Chapter 4

Molly

Freshman Year MIT

"All right, it's Friday, homework is done. You don't have any excuses ..." Brooks waggles his eyebrows as he closes his laptop.

"No excuses for what?" I ask before stacking the books and papers strewn all over my bed.

Since Brooks and I are both studying biomedical engineering, our schedules and classes are really similar. Our English comp professor put us together for the research paper we've been working on all afternoon. We're also lab partners in chemistry. It's like the universe wanted us to be friends, and I'm good with that. Brooks has quickly become my only friend at college.

Besides Todd. But I'm not sure he counts since he goes to Harvard, not MIT.

"We have our very first college party tonight, *and* you're not getting out of it. No excuses!" He hoists his backpack over his shoulder and grabs my hand before trying to drag me from my dorm room.

Dorm room is not the best description though. I've seen a few of the other dorms and mine is by far the most luxurious, with its own kitchenette and bathroom. It's not the *real* college experience. Even my meals are delivered weekly by a service my parents hired to ensure I'm eating healthy, quality food. I suppose this is just how things go when your father has expectations to meet in his social circles.

"And on the way to the party, we're getting ..." he lowers his voice to sound like some kind of evil sorcerer. "McDonald's!" He lets go of my hand to throw his hands in the air and perform an evil laugh.

"Very funny." I place my fists on my hips and glare at him. "It's not my fault I didn't know what McDonald's was. My parents never took me there!"

The second week of school, Brooks asked if I wanted to grab lunch at McDonald's. I'd never heard of it before, so I thought it was a nice restaurant. I even rushed to my dorm after class to change into a sheath dress and heels. Apparently, he'll never let it go.

"What about commercials? Didn't you have a television?" He raises an eyebrow in question.

"Of course we owned a TV." I tug at the collar of my shirt, a nervous habit I've had since I was a child. "We just didn't really watch it much with all our lessons."

"What kind of lessons kept you busy *all* the time?"

I count the lessons with my fingers. "Let's see ... French, Latin, Spanish, tennis, piano ..."

"Okay, okay." He holds his hands up in front of him. "I keep forgetting you live a ritzy life. Which seems to mean you've never had any fun. You already said Todd is busy tonight, so no more sitting in your fancy-schmancy apartment counting your money."

I roll my eyes. "Oh, yeah, that's totally what I do. I also swim around in my gold doubloons like Scrooge McDuck."

Brooks bursts out laughing. "Ah-ha! So you did watch at least *some* TV!"

"One of our nannies allowed me and my sister to turn it on sometimes. Like when my parents were busy entertaining or out of town." I sigh, remembering Gertrude and her fondness for breaking the rules. "She didn't keep her job very long. But it was fun while it lasted."

He grins. "I knew there was a rebel deep down inside that debutante package. Let's go!" He waves an arm and his long legs start walking quickly down the hallway.

I hesitate, but then decide it's okay to have a little fun. And I follow him.

Chapter 5

Brooks

Monday morning, I arrive at the office downtown dressed casually as usual. I'm going to cover up my clothes with my lab coat, anyway. Tan dress pants, long-sleeved Henley, and backwards baseball cap. My signature work look. My mother would have a heart attack if she knew I dressed like this for work. She has high expectations of her children's image. But work is my safe place ... and the one place Diane Windell isn't allowed. She doesn't have clearance. I told her our lab is top secret, employees only ... which is *kind of* true at least. But we're designing medical implants ... not nuclear weapons.

Vanderwin Technologies is the name Molly and I came up for our company. It combines our last names:

Vanderbilt and Windell. Vanderwin has been successful in the last few years since getting FDA approval for our implants. But it's not huge. We rent out the top floor of a three-story building, and, for now, the space suffices. Almost half of the space is for the lab where I design and test products. A quarter is Molly's office, and the rest is an open office space for our half-dozen other employees. Glass separates each space to keep the areas bright and open. I love how I can see the dim, under-cabinet blue lights from the lab as soon as I step foot on the third floor. There's only a thick glass door separating me from the office. I place my thumb on the security scanner and the door beeps, opening automatically.

The first thing I do is look toward Molly's office. Her dark hair is piled on top of her head in a ballerina bun, leaving just her thick bangs hanging down. I can't see her entire outfit, but she's wearing something pink. She glances up, smiling at me before scribbling some notes on the pad in front of her and saying something to whoever she's speaking with.

That smile. It instantly makes my morning brighter. I love working with Molly.

What could be better than working with your best friend? (Besides possibly kissing her).

Hope, a friend Molly met at tennis and one of our very first employees, smiles and greets me at the reception desk. Her friendly smile and bouncy blonde curls make her the picture-perfect receptionist. And she has the work ethic to boot. "Good morning, Mr. Windell!"

I tilt my head and shoot her a mock glare. She knows I hate being called Mr. Windell and does it just to annoy me.

"Good morning, Miss McCully."

She chuckles, then the phone rings and she answers in her chipper voice, "Good morning! Vanderwin Technologies, Hope speaking."

I continue walking and every employee I pass glances up at me from their desks with friendly smiles. I notice Layla, Molly's other tennis friend-turned-medical-sales manager. Her dark hair is pulled back into a no-nonsense ponytail, and my steps slow when I see the goofy smirk on her face.

"What?" I ask, stopping next to her desk.

She shakes her head and busies herself typing on her computer. "Nothing."

Okay ... that was weird.

I walk toward the lab, stopping to scan my thumb print again at the door. It opens and I walk inside, hanging my Patagonia backpack on a peg and grabbing a clean white lab coat.

Pulling my laptop out of my satchel, I open the files I've been working on. Breast and glute implants got us started, but plastic surgery isn't my end goal for Vanderwin Technologies. I glance at my designs for knee replacement surgeries and study it, seeing what I'm missing to make it even more functional. I'm lost in thought until I hear the lab door beep.

Molly walks in smiling, but she seems nervous. Things between me and Molly have always been comfortable and natural, so this isn't normal.

"There's my brilliant best friend!" she says, moving toward me and slapping my shoulder with one hand.

"Okay, let's have it," I swivel on my metal stool to look directly into her big blue eyes. "What do you need?"

"Need? Ha! What would make you think that?" She messes with the collar on her pink dress, her telltale sign of nervousness. "Did I mention you look dashing today?"

I quirk a brow and study her face. I know she's trying to butter me up for whatever mysterious reason, but she's not one to pay compliments to my physical appearance. There's the slightest blush coloring her cheeks now, making me feel a tingle of satisfaction.

"Dashing, huh?"

She gulps slowly and looks down at her pointy-toed shoes before tilting her head back up to look at me.

"Just tell me," I say.

"Okay, I need a favor." Her chest moves up and down with a heavy sigh and I try not to notice. "But before I ask, I want you to know that it's okay for you to say no. There's no pressure at all. No hard feelings."

"Okay." I chuckle. "Just get on with it already."

"I'd also like to remind you of all the English papers I helped you with back in college out of the kindness of my heart, without asking for anything in return."

"Until now?" I tease.

She narrows her eyes at me. "Awfully sassy for someone who didn't know the difference between *there*, *their*, and *they're*."

I scoff and pop the collar on my lab coat. "You see, because of my brilliance in science and mathematics, there's no room up there for all the various adaptations of *there*."

"And what's your excuse for not knowing the difference between the spelling of the deer *doe* and cookie *dough*?" The corner of her mouth turns up slightly.

I match her expression. "You're not very good at buttering people up before asking for a favor."

She sighs. "You're right. I'm sorry. You're the most brilliant, wonderful, amazing, best friend a girl could ask for." She looks at me with big, puppy-dog eyes.

"That's better," I say sarcastically even though I twitch internally every time she refers to me as *friend*.

She grows serious again. "I need a date for my sister's wedding."

I feel the color leave my face and my eyes get wider. Molly Vanderbilt, the girl I've been pining over for years, is asking me to be her date.

And I can't say yes.

"Well," she continues. Her hand goes up once more to play with her collar. "It would be even better if my date was ... like a boyfriend."

I'm not sure how it's possible, but my eyes widen even more. They must be the size of a doe right about now ... The deer doe, not cookie dough.

"Not an actual boyfriend!" she adds, laughing uncomfortably.

The more she speaks, the more confused I become. I hold a hand out in front of me, urging her to stop.

Molly links her hands together behind her back and rocks on her heels like she's in the principal's office getting a lecture.

"Molly, what exactly do you need me to do? This is *me*. I'm not here to judge you. Just tell me what's going on."

She releases a deep breath and unlaces her hands, bringing one to her forehead and rubbing it as if she has a headache. "I know, I'm sorry. My sister is turning me into a lunatic."

Molly sits on the stool right next to me, close enough I can smell her perfume ... Chanel No. 5. Her signature scent. I want to bathe in it.

"Mildred is already bugging me to get back together with Todd and I know my mother will do the same thing …" She bites her bottom lip adorably before continuing. "I thought if I brought a date to the wedding—which she's insisting I do—and everyone thought that date was someone I'm serious about …" she trails off, leaving me to put it all together for myself.

"Like … a boyfriend?"

"Well, yeah. A *fake* boyfriend. And then maybe everyone will stay off my case."

I close my eyes, wishing so badly I could say yes to her request. "Molly, you know I'd do anything for you. Anything." I pause. "But if I break the terms of the bet …"

"I thought you might be worried about that!" She smiles while tapping her index finger on her temple. "But no one at the wedding knows about the bet. And besides my parents, my sister, and Todd … no one will even know who you are." She waggles her eyebrows, making me laugh.

I remove my baseball cap and run a hand through my hair with a groan. "If my brothers were to find out, they would literally make me run naked through my mother's garden party. You realize that, right? David wasn't kidding. The man is sadistic."

Her shoulders slump in disappointment for a moment before she straightens them again. "Yeah, yeah.

You're right! Sorry for even bringing it up." She smiles, but I can see the disappointment in her eyes.

"Molly—" I start, but she interrupts me.

"No, really! I'm fine." She stands and places a manicured hand on my shoulder and pats it a few times. "I'll see you at lunch?"

Her voice sounds high and strained, and I can tell she's holding back how she truly feels. She'd do anything to keep everyone happy, even at the expense of her own feelings. Which is why she's looking for a fake boyfriend ... and always getting back together with Todd.

"Yeah, see you at lunch." I smile and she turns to leave. "Hey, Molly?"

She glances over her shoulder as she pulls the door open to leave. "Yeah?"

"I'll think about it, okay?"

Her eyes widen, and she smiles her genuine smile. "Okay!"

Molly and I head to one of our favorite lunch places that serves the best soup and sandwiches. It's called Soup'r Sandwiches. Not very original ... but at least the food is good. We go for a late lunch every Monday. This allows her to catch me up on the business side of Vanderwin ... but we mostly end up chatting about non-business related topics.

We order at the shabby-chic wooden bar area, then Molly grabs a table for us while I wait for our orders. I'm at ease and looking forward to our lunch despite disappointing her earlier today. But out of nowhere, I feel like a dark cloud is looming over me. My skin prickles and the hair on the back of my neck stand on end. Glancing over my shoulder, I see Turd Da Punk.

Er, Todd Du Pont.

His saccharine smile is aimed at me, completely ignoring the blonde woman next to him. She has her arm linked around his and is looking up at him like he's the best thing since sliced bread. Actually, sliced bread is lame ... How about the best thing since Vanderwin Technologies glute implants?

"Brooks, what a pleasure to see you here," Todd says in a low voice, like he's trying to sound more masculine or something.

I nod at Todd and send his date a friendly smile. She blushes before loosening her grip on Todd's arm and doing a little hair flip. Her gaze on me is awfully flirtatious for someone who was looking at another guy with such admiration five seconds ago. I look away from her, not wanting to give her any ideas. This is the problem with being friendly; women think I'm flirting even when I'm not.

"Monday *business* lunch with Molly?" Todd asks, oblivious to the woman on his arm giving me bedroom eyes. He draws out the word business, like it's a curse word.

"Yes, I'm sure you remember this is one of her favorite cafes," I tell him, narrowing my eyes slightly so he knows I see right through his charade. Like, he just randomly brought this woman to one of Molly's favorite places on a day and time we were likely to be here ... Yeah, I wasn't born yesterday, Todd.

Molly must have gotten curious about what was taking so long and I see her walking toward me. She's smiling, but there's a question in her expression ... until she spots Todd and the blonde.

Molly reaches us and stands next to me. Her body is rigid and I can sense she's uncomfortable. Oh, and there goes her hand to her collar, toying with the edge.

"Molly!" Todd says in a surprised tone, which is obviously fake. "This is Trudy. She's my date to Preston and Mildred's wedding. So glad we ran into you so we could get this awkwardness out of the way."

He looks at Molly like he pities her and something inside me cracks open. I wrap an arm around Molly's waist and pull her into my side. I chuckle and then send Todd a faux grimace. "Yes, this definitely saves some awkwardness at the wedding—because I'll be there too. I'm Molly's date."

I'm like the handsome version of the incredible Hulk, breaking apart to save my woman. Okay, I *wish* she was my woman. But as of two seconds ago, she *is* my fake girlfriend ... and nobody messes with my fake girlfriend.

Todd's eyes widen slightly before he forces a smile on his face. But his nostrils are flaring, so I know I'm getting to him.

I glance down at Molly, who's still nestled against me. She fits perfectly, just like I always knew she would. Her cheeks pinken as she looks up at me with wide eyes. A smirk tugs at my lips, and I wink at her, urging her to play along.

Her eyes twinkle when realization hits her that this is me agreeing to be her wedding date ... despite the embarrassing repercussion if my brothers find out.

She giggles and brings a hand up to my chest. "I'm so happy we both have dates and this won't be weird."

She smiles at Todd and his date. Trudy grins back at her before clapping her hands together gleefully. "Oh, how fun! Maybe we can go on a double date!"

Todd's head whips over to his date. His face has horror written all over it. Molly's hand starts to slip away from my chest, but I grab it with my free hand to keep it there. Resting right over my heart.

Todd catches the movement and focuses on us again. "So, you two finally got together, huh?"

"Yeah, we went on our first official date Saturday. And we have another one planned for tonight." I release my hand from Molly's and boop her nose playfully.

She rolls her lips together like she's trying not to laugh. "Oh yes, I can't wait for tonight. It's so sweet of you to plan our dates *and* remember them." Her face pales as soon as the words leave her mouth, like she's shocked she said that outloud.

"I could never forget you, sugar bear." I kiss the top of her head, allowing my lips to linger for a few seconds. The subtle, feminine scent of her shampoo is making me weak in the knees. I have to force myself to remove my mouth and nose from her hair.

I risk another glance at Todd and Trudy. Trudy is scrolling through her phone, looking bored. But Todd has a maniacal smile on his face, his nostrils still flaring wildly.

Molly grabs my arm gently. "Oh, silly us! Our food has been sitting here getting cold."

I chuckle and turn to get the tray that holds our chicken salad croissant sandwiches and tomato basil soup. "Well, great seeing you guys," I say confidently before turning and walking away.

"See you at the wedding!" Molly calls over her shoulder as she follows me, looping her arm through mine.

I could definitely get used to her touching me so much.

Chapter 6

Molly

I watch Todd and Trudy grab their order and promptly leave the cafe. Todd is basically dragging the poor girl along behind him.

The laugh I've been holding back for ten minutes frees itself from my mouth and Brooks breaks into laughter as well.

"What just happened?" I ask him, breathless from laughing.

He shrugs one muscular shoulder, which makes my brain flick back to the feeling of his hard chest beneath my hand. Todd's chest definitely never felt that firm. How does Brooks find the time to work out? I know how often he works late into the night.

"I think I just became your fake boyfriend." His bright blue eyes twinkle mischievously as he takes a bite from his sandwich.

I shake my head, smiling. "But why? What made you change your mind?"

He swallows, and his expression turns serious. He reaches across the table like he's going to hold my hand, but something passes over his expression and he pulls his hand back. "Molly, I wasn't about to let that jerk parade around with *Trampy Trudy*." He wrinkles his nose as he says her name. "I will always be the guy on your side. Protecting you ... whatever you need. A stupid bet won't change that."

There's a rush of nerves deep in my stomach that performs a little somersault at his words, and the look he's giving me. Brooks always has a jovial look about him with his boy next door vibe ... but there's something darker and more sultry about the way he's looking at me now. Something I haven't seen ... or noticed before.

Sweat creeps onto my upper lip. Why is that always the first place to sweat when nervous? So unattractive. I reach for my drink as a distraction. Brooks is still looking at me causing me to miss my straw twice. I'm sure I look like a moron. I finally catch my straw and take a sip.

One corner of his mouth flinches slightly, like he's amused. We eat silently for several minutes before I finally speak. "So, I'm guessing you have some formal wear, or a tux? If not, I'll buy you something."

He chuckles. "You've met my mother. *The* one and only Diane Windell. Of course I own a tux. Actually, I have a copious amount of formal attire."

"How about a black suit with a red tie?"

"I'm sure I have at least a dozen red ties." He grins.

"God bless you, Diane," I tease, drawing a laugh from Brooks. "That will be perfect. My dress is red."

"We'll be the picture-perfect couple." He winks. "So, do I need to book a hotel?"

I wave his comment off with my hand. "My parent's cabin in Vermont is ... generous in size. There will be plenty of room for you." I'm used to wording things in such a way to play down my parent's wealth, but their cabin is more than generous. It's a literal mansion. If the front wasn't constructed of logs, you'd never be able to refer to it as a cabin.

"All right. I'm kind of excited to finally see it."

I smile fondly. "It's one of my favorite places. If it wasn't so peaceful and quiet out there, I probably wouldn't be able to tolerate Christmases with my family." I sigh. "It won't really be the same with a hundred wedding guests—and my sister—terrorizing the place."

His lips twist in a comical way, somewhere between a smirk and a grimace. "Well, at least I'll be there to keep you company."

I smile back, feeling a sense of calm wash over me. Sometime in the last six years, my best friend went from an arrogant boy to a caring man. A man who is putting my needs ahead of his own. It's quite touching.

And knowing he'll be there makes me feel so much better already.

That evening, I arrive home from work and slip my heels off the moment I walk through my front door. I'm juggling my large Fendi laptop bag, a water bottle, and my car keys when my phone pings three times in a row.

It never fails that my phone goes off the moment my hands are full. Could it have been blowing up while I was sitting at my desk earlier? Of course not.

Setting my items down in the built-in cubby by my door, I pull my phone out of my purse. A myriad of texts from Mildred appear. I close my eyes and take a deep breath before opening and reading them.

Mildred: Todd told Preston you found a date for the wedding?

Mildred: Please let me know who it is ASAP.

Mildred: I need to make sure your date will go with the wedding aesthetic.

Mildred: I know you rolled your eyes at that ... but wedding photos last FOREVER.

She's right. I did roll my eyes. Walking down the slim hallway from my front door into my kitchen, I grab a long-stemmed wine glass and a bottle of red wine from one of my favorite wineries in Napa. I pour myself a large glass and take a few sips—er, gulps—before responding to my sister.

Molly: My date is Brooks Windell. You remember meeting him at my college graduation?
Mildred: Oh. You're just bringing a friend? Well, at least he's gorgeous. Brooks will be perfect to make Todd jealous and come crawling back to you.
Molly: Well, actually ... Brooks and I are recently romantically involved. And I don't want Todd back, remember?
Mildred: Umm ... it must be very recent ... since you JUST broke up with Todd like four days ago!?

I shake my head that she didn't bat an eyelash extension when Todd had a date for the wedding two days ago, but now she's freaked out about *me* dating someone? At least I waited until the relationship was over, unlike Todd. And my "boyfriend" isn't even a real boyfriend. Not that I'm going to tell my perfect sister that.

Biting my bottom lip, I try to remember the details Brooks made up earlier.

Molly: Yep. Went on our first date Saturday night and going out again tonight. He was there for me after the breakup. Actually, he's always been there for me.

At least that last part isn't a lie. Brooks really is always there to be a proverbial shoulder to cry on. And what a solid shoulder it is.

Stop thinking like that, Molly. One feel of his chest muscles and my brain has been compromised.

Mildred: Hm, okay. Well, at least you have a date. And he'll look great in pictures.

I narrow my eyes at her text and don't bother responding. After that text exchange, I decide it's best to turn off my phone, have wine for dinner, and take a long, hot bubble bath. One of my favorite things we did during the remodel was creating the perfect master bathroom. Much to my contractor's chagrin, I had him tear down a wall and convert a whole bedroom into my walk-in closet and luxury bathroom complete with an antique clawfoot bathtub.

No regrets.

Carrying my glass of wine up the curved staircase, I manage to get the back of my dress unzipped with one hand. I make it to my bedroom at the top of the steps and peel off the rest of my clothes before walking to the bathroom and starting the bath.

I slide into the tub and sigh as the hot water makes the stress of the day slip away. The bath salts my mother sent from Paris fill the room with the scent of roses. I breathe in the aroma before sinking a little deeper into the tub.

In my head, I go through the events of the past few days. A melancholy feeling settles over me when I think back to Friday night. I went from looking forward to a night out with Todd to breaking up with him. Todd was my first kiss, and the first man I said *I love you* to. And there was a part of me who thought he'd be the last, too. But somewhere beneath that sad feeling, there's also a sense of relief. Or maybe freedom? It's been kind of nice not having to talk to him each evening and hear him drone on about his job and how he hates Kansas. Oh, and how his friends back in Massachusetts are leading more exciting lives than him.

Todd really despises living in Kansas. But then why'd he follow me here? Obviously, he never took our relationship seriously, so why not stay in Massachusetts with his family and friends?

Back in college, I hoped Todd might follow me here when Brooks and I decided to start our own company. But I never asked him to. Honestly, I thought we'd do the long distance thing until we eventually got married. And I never really thought much past that. I pictured him proposing, and maybe a wedding, but nothing further into the future than that. Not growing old together, or having children, or vacationing in the Maldives. And you should probably daydream about all of those things with the person you want to marry.

But me and Todd just stayed together, regardless. I think I stayed out of a sense of duty to my mother. But why did Todd stay with me? Maybe he didn't want to make things awkward. I'm not even sure anymore.

My bathwater has started to cool, so I get out and wrap myself in a fluffy white towel that has a cursive V monogrammed on it. A house warming gift from my mother. She has never come to Kansas to visit me, but she'll send expensive gifts in lieu of actually spending quality time with me. With a heavy sigh, I walk to my dresser and start to grab some sleep shorts and a t-shirt before changing my mind and selecting a pretty little nightgown instead. Just because I'm single doesn't mean I can't feel good about myself.

I slip the light pink silk over my head and let it drape over my body. The spaghetti straps don't offer much in the way of warmth, but after another glass of wine,

I'll warm up. I quickly comb out my damp hair before finding my now-empty wine glass and heading back down the stairs.

When I get to the kitchen, I ask my Bluetooth device to shuffle music by Post Malone— my guilty pleasure. (My mother would fall over dead if she knew.) Then I refill my wine glass.

I'm shaking my booty, sipping wine, and rapping along with every word when I hear a throat clearing behind me. I nearly jump out of my skin and shriek so loud it feels like my eardrums will burst.

"Ahhh!" I turn and see Brooks standing in my kitchen, a bag of takeout in one hand and a bouquet of flowers in the other.

His eyebrows are so high they're practically part of his hairline. "I tried calling, but you didn't answer, so I used my key."

"Alexa, stop music!" I yell at the blaring Bluetooth device. "Sorry, I took a bath and turned my phone off so my sister couldn't bother me." It hits me for the first time that even Brooks and I exchanged keys to each other's homes, but Todd never gave me one. That alone says a lot.

His face relaxes and his eyes drop down to my body for a few seconds, just long enough for me to remember I'm wearing nothing but a slinky nightie.

Brooks leans against the kitchen counter like he's completely unbothered by the situation. He even smirks at me and raises his eyebrows slightly.

If it weren't for the blush coloring his high cheekbones and the tips of his ears, I might actually believe he wasn't the least bit uncomfortable at the sight of me in a barely-there nightgown.

For a moment, I'm so amused by him blushing—since I've *never* seen this man blush before—that I almost forget I'm showing way too much skin. If *I* made him blush, this dating ban must really be getting to him. I'm pretty sure I'm not even his type ... just like he isn't mine.

I cross my arms over my chest for modesty. "So, what are you doing here? Not that you're not welcome anytime."

He laughs nervously, his eyes dropping down to my bare legs briefly before looking down at his feet. "We had a date tonight, remember, schmoopsie poo?" He looks up at me through his thick lashes, that permanent glint of mischief in his eyes.

That look right there is probably what gets all the ladies swooning over him.

I huff out a laugh. "You were serious about that?"

He shrugs a shoulder. "We need to be convincing, right? Plus, we have to eat anyway."

"True." I look down at my legs, where his eyes seem to keep looking, and suddenly my nightie feels much shorter than it did when I put it on earlier. "I'm going to run upstairs and change … Go ahead and get some wine if you want!"

I make a run for the stairs and he's gentlemanly enough not to watch my unbecoming half-run.

Chapter 7

Brooks

Molly isn't upstairs long enough for me to grasp what I just saw. The wild dance moves, the fact that she knows every word to Post Malone's latest rap song ... And then, of course, those smooth legs and the tiny nightgown that looked so soft. Let's not forget her hair falling down her back ... still wet. A strangled whimper escapes my mouth.

Hell, even just the scent of her fresh out of the bath has my body on fire ... that subtle yet luxurious herbal scent. I wanted to push her up against the counter and kiss her until both of us were breathless ... to feel her skin against mine ... to tangle my fingers in her wet hair ...

Unfortunately, she sees me as a friend, and that would have been entirely unwelcome. I'm going to have to tread very carefully with this fake boyfriend thing, or I'll get swept away.

Molly returns quickly, now wearing black leggings, fuzzy slippers, and an MIT sweatshirt. Honestly, it's just as hot as the nightgown. I gulp slowly and try not to drool.

"Sorry again for not answering my phone." She laughs, running a hand through her damp hair. "Thanks for bringing dinner. You totally didn't need to do that. I'm not a high maintenance fake girlfriend." She grabs a wine glass and fills it for me.

I laugh at her comment. "Whew, good. Because I got hamburgers and not escargot," I tell her, lifting up a styrofoam container.

"Best fake boyfriend ever!" She grabs the container with a cheesy grin on her makeup-free face. Her skin looks pink and shiny since she just washed her face and probably put all kinds of goop on it the way girls do.

We carry our food and wine into the living room where she has a modern loveseat and sofa in a light pink velvet. Molly has her own eclectic style that I love. Her antique spoon collection is displayed proudly above her mantle. Seeing some of the spoons I've given her over the years fills me with pride. I don't think she's ever even considered that I've been the one randomly sending her spoons over the years. Watercolor paintings hang on each side of the spoon display, one of Vermont in the winter, and the other of Massachusetts in the fall.

Her home is such a random mixture of old and new that somehow fit perfectly together. Her house is a reflection of herself: an old soul who can still get on board with new ideas.

I make myself comfortable on the sofa next to her, but not close enough to be touching or even accidentally brushing arms. Not sure I trust myself after the whole nightgown debacle.

Molly picks up her burger and takes a large bite of it, causing ketchup to drip out the bottom. "Yum. This is probably the best date ever." She nudges me with her elbow.

I laugh, but can't help but wish this was really a date, that she was really mine, that I had really given her the best date of her life.

"Not bad for a second date …" I rub my chin with my hand like I'm deep in thought. "Might even take you on a third date."

She chuckles and dabs at her lips with a paper napkin before taking a sip of her wine. "Well, my sister's wedding is in a week and a half so … you kind of have to."

Popping a french fry into my mouth, I chew and swallow quickly before clearing my throat. "Speaking of the wedding ... I thought maybe we should have some ground rules." I shoot her a tense smile.

She quirks a brow. "You? Rules? Who are you and what have you done with Brooks?"

I huff out a laugh. "Yeah, I know. But I want to keep this pretty low-key with the bet and all."

Molly sets her food down and gives me her full attention. "Okay, what were you thinking?"

"Well, we can't touch each other or I'll break the rules of the bet."

She sighs. "Brooks ... how is anyone going to believe you're my new boyfriend if we won't even touch each other?"

I rub the back of my neck, feeling stressed. I know the likelihood of my brothers finding out about this are slim to none ... but if I start holding Molly's hand ... or actually *kiss* her, I'm not sure I'll ever recover.

"That's true." I concede. "So maybe a few dances and brief hand-holding?"

She studies me for a moment before responding. "Three slow dances, unlimited hand-holding ... and flirting."

"*Unlimited*??" I bring my hand to my chest like I'm scandalized. "Molly Vanderbilt, are you trying to take away my innocence?"

She pinches my arm and I rub the spot dramatically.

"*You*? Innocent?" She rolls her eyes, but she's smiling.

I chuckle but then look away from her and study the art on the wall. "But like ... no kissing, right?" I look back at her again.

"Oh my gosh, does the thought of kissing me seem that gross?" She laughs, but there's something in her eyes that looks slightly offended.

"No. It doesn't," I say with conviction, the words slipping out before I can stop them. She holds my gaze for a moment, a question in her expression. I try to lighten the mood with a laugh, but it sounds strangled. "It's just ... you're my best friend and I don't want anything to be weird between us."

Her shoulders relax like she'd been holding her breath. "Yeah, that's a good point. Okay, no kissing."

We finish our burgers and wine in silence. Silence between us is usually comfortable and not weird at all. But this silence feels so quiet there's a ringing in my ears. And it's somehow charged with something I can't quite name. It's all just ... different than usual.

"So, how are the knee replacement designs coming along?" She breaks the silence, and I feel relieved.

Work is something we can always talk about, because we will always have that in common. "Really good, actually. I still have some kinks to work out in the design. I want it to feel like a real knee, to move seamlessly and comfortably. It's the most challenging thing I've attempted so far."

She nods. "Yeah, I bet. But if anyone can do it, you can."

My heart speeds up inside my chest, because I know she truly believes in me. Not because of my last name, or my family's money. Not because she wants anything from me, but simply because she respects me as a person and is proud to be my friend.

And this is where my feelings become complicated ... Besides my family, she's the only one who I feel both respects me and really *gets* me. Honestly, even my siblings think I'm just a womanizing goofball most of the time.

Her genuine respect makes my desire for her even stronger. And yet, it makes the thought of expressing my feelings and ruining our friendship even more excruciating.

Chapter 8

Brooks

Sophomore Year MIT

Walking up to Molly's dorm room to work on our lab project, I stop outside her door and take a deep breath. Maybe if I prepare myself ahead of time to see her pretty face, kind smile, and grand-millennial style—that for some reason is so sexy to me—my heart won't leap outside of my chest the way it always seems to when I'm around her.

But I know there's nothing I can do to avoid the fluttery feeling. I've tried everything. Including reminding myself a billion times that she has a boyfriend. And speaking of billion ... that's how many dollars he has. (Or at least his family does.)

My family may have millions, but there's a vast difference between millionaires and billionaires—just ask Dave Ramsey. And aside from the money, there are deep family ties between her family and Todd's ... and that's something I definitely can't compete with.

I tap on the door with bated breath and when Molly whisks the door open, my heart stops and not for the normal reasons, but because she's been crying. Her eyes are puffy and her face is red.

She tries, unsuccessfully, to smile. "Oh, hey, Brooks! I forgot about our research paper ... Come on in." She moves to the side to let me in.

I step inside the spacious dorm room. Molly doesn't have a roommate: perks of one of the libraries on campus having your last name in the title. She has enough room for a queen-size canopy bed. The bed frame is brass, and it looks like a family heirloom. Her antique spoon collection—which I love to make fun of, but secretly think is really cool—is hung on the wall next to her bed. The other walls are lined with art, but it's all very classy and aesthetically pleasing ... not your typical boy band posters like in the other girls' dorm rooms.

She follows me inside and sits on the edge of her bed. I take a seat on the plush white rug on the floor, sitting criss-cross applesauce.

"So, you gonna tell me what's wrong?" I say playfully, with a quirk of one eyebrow.

She laughs, but her eyes are sad. "Todd and I broke up this morning. He said he wanted freedom to enjoy being young ... or something like that."

I scoff at the idea of wanting freedom from Molly. This girl is the ultimate package. "Well, then he's an idiot and you're better off without him."

She sighs and sniffs. I grab the tissues from the desk right behind me and toss them to her. "Thanks." She smiles then dabs her eyes and blows her nose. "It's not that simple though. Our families are so close. We vacation together ... spend holidays together. I just feel like Todd and I are *meant to be*, you know?"

My heart feels like someone is grabbing it and twisting. Hearing her say those words with such conviction doesn't give me much hope for anything ever developing past friendship between her and I.

But I'd rather be her friend than be nothing at all ... so with all the strength I can muster, I say something that's hopefully encouraging. "Yeah. I bet he'll come to his senses soon."

"Thanks, I hope you're right." She smiles, looking a little more like herself now. "You're such a good friend."

I smile back at her, but the word *friend* reverberates in my mind over and over again like a curse. I've never been friend zoned in my entire life ... never been turned down by a female. And the *one girl* I truly want is the first one to do it.

So I'll continue being her friend and do some antiquing tomorrow to look for spoons. That's one way I know to brighten up her bad days: get her a new antique spoon for her collection. I always attach an anonymous note to it and laugh that she can't ever seem to figure out who it's from. Todd usually gets credit for the spoons ... which is annoying.

But I keep doing it anyway.

Maybe someday she'll put the pieces together. Then perhaps she'll see I'm the one who really sees her, really understands her ... really wants her to be mine.

Chapter 9

Molly

I find a small red box on my desk when I arrive at work the next day. The box is wrapped in white ribbon with a note attached to it. By the handwriting, I can tell it's going to be an antique spoon for my collection from my infamous secret admirer.

Why does Todd bother? Anytime I have a bad day or we break up, he sends me a spoon and it tugs at my heartstrings.

My grandmother gave me my first spoon when I was born. It's a small, silver polished spoon with a little kitten engraved in the handle. Yes ... I was literally born with a silver spoon. The irony is not lost on me.

Curiosity gets the best of me and I rip open the box before reading the note.

The strangest things about Todd sending me a spoon at a time like this is:

1. He's with Trudy.

2. He has always made fun of my spoon collection and told me it's stupid.

He never even showed any interest in antiquing with me … so where does he find the spoons?

Well, sorry, Todd. You're not spooning your way into my heart this time, buddy. Save your overrated spoons for Trudy. I pull the lid off the box and gasp. Okay, I may keep this one after all. Trudy can have the next one.

I pull a shiny golden spoon out of the box. It has an intricately engraved handle, and crystals are embedded throughout along with small red stones that look like rubies.

"Wow," I whisper to myself.

"Wow, what?" Layla's voice comes from my open office door, making me jump and nearly drop my new spoon.

Layla walks over to see what I'm holding, and I hand her the fabulous little spoon and then read the note.

Molly,
You're like this spoon … classically beautiful, but unique.
You stand out from all the others.
Love,

Your Secret Admirer

"This is so beautiful! Is it from the infamous secret admirer?" Layla asks, twirling the spoon and admiring it.

Layla's comment makes me chuckle and I look up from the note, shaking my head at her. "Yep." I say, holding the note up so she can see it.

"And you've been getting them since college, right?" she asks, taking the note from my hand and reading it with a smile.

I nod. "Yep. They always show up after I've had a horrible day or Todd and I have broken up."

She considers my words for a moment. "So you think it's Todd trying to win you back?"

"It has to be Todd. I can't think of anyone else."

She studies the note again. "I'd think it was Brooks, but this isn't his handwriting."

Briefly, I wonder if it could be Brooks. But the thought passes quickly. Brooks has known me for years and has never expressed romantic interest. Even when Todd and I broke up, he only ever treated me like a friend. He doesn't try to be physically affectionate with me, and he dates women by the dozen. *Gorgeous* women.

I shake my head. "I'm sure the spoons will stop arriving once Todd realizes I won't give him any more chances."

She hands the note back to me.

Brooks pops his head inside my office. He looks like he just got here. "Good morning, ladies!" he says cheerfully. "What do you have there?" He looks at the red box, his expression completely neutral.

"Another antique spoon," I say evenly, watching his face for any clues that it could be from him.

"No way. You're still getting those?" He huffs out a small laugh.

Yep, definitely not Brooks.

"Yeah ... if Todd is the one sending them to me, I hope he's not expecting me to crawl back to him." I eye the spoon admirably once more. "Although this is the prettiest spoon yet, I have to admit."

Brooks takes a few strides into the room and takes the spoon from me. His large masculine hands make the spoon look minuscule. Like King Kong carrying that blonde lady ... one of the many films I was introduced to by Brooks.

His eyebrows raise slightly. "Wow, this one's nice. I wonder how old it is?"

"It looks like maybe the Art Deco time period?" Layla says, looking straight at Brooks like she's trying to get a read on him.

He nods in agreement and hands the spoon back to me. "Yeah, you're right I think." He gives a small, one-shoulder shrug.

I tuck the spoon inside its box before putting it in my purse. "I'm going to need a new spoon rack," I tell them. "Which gives me a great excuse to go antiquing. Brooks, let's go in Vermont! They have some great shops."

Brooks is always up for antiquing with me. Actually, he's always up for anything.

He glances awkwardly toward Layla and I laugh. "It's okay; Layla and Hope know all about our ruse."

He huffs out a relieved sigh. "Okay whew. I wasn't sure who all was in on this whole conspiracy."

Layla narrows her eyes at Brooks and crosses her arms. "You better take good care of our girl. I know where you work."

"I'll be the best fake boyfriend I can be," he says seriously before grinning and walking toward the door. "Well, I'm off to my lair. Have a good day, ladies." He sends me a sweet smile once more before walking to the lab.

Layla looks at me. "How can you friend zone that poor man?"

I scoff. "You're ridiculous. Get back to work." I snap my fingers, but then give her a playful smile.

She rolls her eyes and heads back to her desk.

She's just trying to get a reaction from me. Surely she can see that Brooks didn't seem the least bit guilty when he saw the spoon. His expression was neutral, maybe slightly amused. If Brooks had feelings for me, I would've realized it *sometime* over the last six years.

Layla has obviously been watching too many romantic Christmas movies.

Chapter 10

Brooks

Friday after work, I'm walking outside to my truck when my phone rings in my pocket. I answer, already knowing it's my mom. I set a special ringtone for her: *Glamorous* by Fergie. She would hate it, but it makes me laugh every time she calls.

I answer the phone as I walk. "This is the Kansas State Penitentiary. Press one to receive a call from your loved one."

Mom sighs on the other line. "Can you ever just answer the phone normally?"

I laugh. "Where's the fun in that?" She doesn't answer. "So, how's the most important woman in my life?"

"I'm good, sweetheart," she says, and I can hear the smile in her voice. The *most important woman* title always perks her up. "I'm calling to see if you'd like to invite Molly to family dinner tomorrow?"

My face falls. Over the years I've carefully kept Molly all to myself. Partially because I'm a selfish pig and don't want to share. And also because if they saw me with her, it'd be obvious to them that I have feelings for her.

Don't get me wrong; I love my family and how close we are ... but the downside is that they know me too well. I've contemplated asking Molly to come with me on holidays since she doesn't have family nearby, but I always decide against it. Thankfully, she spends most holidays in Massachusetts or Vermont. When she's in Kansas over a holiday, Hope and Layla always invite her to go with them.

"Uh, sure I could ... but why exactly?"

"Well, it's just ..." her voice cracks with emotion. "Madden and Odette will be in D.C... and David and Isa are abroad..." she sniffles. "The table is going to feel so empty without everyone. It's just so hard watching my children move away."

I frown. Diane Windell isn't a crier ... She's strict, tough-love, and critical. I'm not sure if she's faking it, but the idea of her crying breaks down my defenses quickly. "It's weird without them for sure. I'm sorry, Mom."

She sniffs again. "It's okay. I just thought if we invited some more guests, the table would seem full, you know?"

"Yeah, okay ... I'll ask Molly." I've made it to my truck now and lean against it with a resigned slump.

"Oh, wonderful!" she says in an excited tone, but her voice still sounds a little shakier than I've heard it in a long time. "We'll see you tomorrow then?"

"Yeah, of course. Love you, Mom."

"Love you too." Her voice sounds steadier now, and I hear crinkling. I wonder if she's breaking into her secret stash of chocolate. She stores it inside the crockpot in the kitchen cabinet. "Oh, and Brooks?"

"Yeah, Mom?"

"Please don't move away."

I choke back a laugh. "I can't. My company is here." And where my company is, Molly is also.

"Thank goodness for that. See you tomorrow." She hangs up, and I wish I could give her a big hug.

Unlocking the driver-side door, I climb inside the truck and turn the key in the ignition. I immediately blast the air conditioning. Yes, it's December. But our office is mostly women, and for some reason, they're always cold. They keep the heat up so high, I practically roast there all day.

I enjoy the feel of the AC blowing in my hair before deciding it's in my best interest to secure my mom's dinner guest. I type out a text to Molly.

Brooks: Hey schmoopsie poo! I think it's time you meet my family. *GIF of Kip from Napoleon Dynamite saying, *I guess you could say things are getting pretty serious**

Molly: Um, what?

Brooks: My mom invited you to family dinner tomorrow.

Molly: *GIF of Jennifer Lawrence receiving an Oscar* Wow. I'm truly honored.

Brooks: You should be. *GIF of men in suits rolling out a red carpet*

Brooks: But seriously, are you free tomorrow? Around 6?

Molly: I don't have any plans! What should I bring?

Brooks: I want to say nothing, but then I know you'll stress about what to bring. So, how about a bottle of wine?

Molly: *wink emoji* You know me too well.

The next evening, I stop by Molly's house to pick her up for family dinner. I walk up the familiar creaky steps to the wrap-around front porch, and her front door whisks open before I can knock.

"Are you sure it's okay I'm coming with you?"

I smile. "Of course. I'm the one who invited you."

Taking in Molly from head to toe, I gulp slowly. She's wearing a black sweater dress, leather Chanel belt and matching knee-high leather boots. I nearly drool at the sight of her. How she can manage to be completely covered—in an extremely classy outfit—and still make me want to blush, is an equation I'll never be able to solve. It's as confusing to me as the three different *theres.*

I'm looking forward to spending the evening with Molly. How could I not be? But I'm also anxious. If anyone can see right through me, it would be my sister, Sophie. Honestly, even her husband, Drew, is weirdly in sync with his emotions. He might be able to read my feelings for my best friend as well.

"Okay." She takes a deep breath and smooths her hands down the front of her dress. "Do I look all right? Your mom makes me nervous."

Trying to keep my facial expression even and friendly, I say, "You look great. Let's go."

She chuckles then ducks inside quickly to grab her coat and a bottle of Sauvignon Blanc. "I'm excited, actually. Your family is so fun. Even though Diane is a little terrifying." She hands me the wine and tugs the coat on as we walk toward my truck. "What do I call her? Ma'am? Mrs. Windell? Diane? Her Royal Highness, Duchess of Wichita?"

"She'd probably prefer that last one."

Molly follows closely behind me as we walk into my parents' dining room. It's warm with a fire blazing in the fireplace. I feel myself starting to sweat already and remove my nice sweater, leaving me in just my white t-shirt. The fireplace doesn't usually make me uncomfortably warm. Dad must've added more logs than usual. It definitely has *nothing* to do with my nervousness at having Molly here with me.

The large, oval table is set with the finest china, the white tablecloth is ironed, and tall candles are lit at the center of the table. It's inviting like it always is, but much fancier than usual.

Molly says my mom makes her nervous... but I'm pretty sure the feeling is mutual. Diane Windell isn't accustomed to being around people who are wealthier than her.

Drew, Sophie, and their girls, Samantha and Penny, are seated at the table. The table is covered in an array of serving platters. My mouth waters as I observe the spread. Sauteed green beans, beef stroganoff, homemade rolls, and a vanilla cake covered with pretty frosting flowers.

Penny spots us first and leaps up from her seat. "Uncle Brooksy!" She flies toward me with the biggest jump she can manage. I leap forward quickly and catch her, then hang her upside down from her feet and tickle her.

She laughs and wriggles, trying to get away. Sammy girl doesn't want to be left out, and she runs toward us, giggling loudly.

"Uncle Bwooksy!" She screeches in her adorable little lisp. I notice the girls are wearing matching pink dresses that have a cutesy reindeer pattern.

A-freaking-dorable.

I throw Penny over my shoulder and use my free arm to hoist Sammy up too. Pretending I lost them, I spin in a circle as if looking for something. Then I rush over to Molly.

"Molly! I can't find my nieces!"

She plays along and gasps in horror. "Oh no! Do you think they're under the table?"

I squat down, making the girls giggle and scream at the sudden movement. "Nope. Not there."

Molly places her hands on her hips, and I notice how great her body looks in that figure-hugging sweater dress. I shake the thought.

"Maybe behind the chairs?" Molly asks, still pretending she can't see them. The girls laugh, and I can hear Drew and Sophie snicker as well.

I bound over to the armchairs in front of the fireplace, making sure to jiggle the girls as much as possible with my movements. "Not here either," I say in a worried voice. "Drew. I'm so sorry for losing the girls."

Drew sighs heavily. "Our house will be lonely without them. But I forgive you."

The girls' laughter gets louder still. "Daddy! We're up here!" Sammy says through bouts of giggles.

"Oh my gosh! I completely forgot I put you guys up there!" I set them on the ground and squat down to pull them into a hug. "Girls, this is my friend Molly."

I gesture behind me where Molly is standing. Drew and Sophie stand and come over toward us.

"Molly! I haven't seen you in ages!" Sophie pulls her into a big hug.

"I know! Brooks is ashamed of me, I think. Wants to keep you all to himself," Molly says with a chuckle.

Drew gives her a side hug. "Nice to see you again. We met a few months ago, before you moved."

"Oh, right! You have the garage gym."

"Yep, that's me! How's the new house?"

"I love it. The remodel took a few months, but now it feels like home."

"Is Mowwy your wife?" Sammy asks, her little brow furrowing.

We all laugh. "No, she's not. We're friends and we work together," I explain.

Penny crosses her arms and looks between me and Molly with a skeptical expression. "Are you going to *make* her your wife, though?"

Drew pats her on the head and casually places one of his hands over her mouth. "Anyway ... really glad you're here for family dinner. It's not usually this fancy."

Molly smiles like she's trying not to laugh. My parents enter the room from the kitchen. Dad is carrying a bottle of wine in each hand, and Mom has a Christmassy floral arrangement.

"Oh, you're here!" Mom sets the flowers on the table near the candles and then fusses with her sweater. "Thanks for joining us, Molly!"

Dad looks grouchy but manages a small smile. "Welcome to our home."

He gives Mom a weird look that makes me wonder if they'd just been arguing in the kitchen. Probably.

"Thank you for having me. Your home is gorgeous," Molly says, glancing around the room.

My parents' house is old, so, of course, Molly would love it. She's been here with me before, but only for brief errands. She's never seen this much of the inside.

"Of course!" My mother preens at her compliment. "Everything is ready, so go ahead and have a seat." She gestures toward the table and we all sit down.

Dad sits at the head of the table and Mom is on his right-hand side. Sophie is on his left, Drew beside her.

The girls are next to him, so I take a seat next to Mom and Molly sits beside me.

It feels good to have her here with my family. It's all too easy for me to picture spending every family dinner with her ... watching her interact with my family ... living our lives together. And that thought is just another reason why I never bring her to family dinners. The last thing I need is my feelings for her becoming even stronger than they already are. But we're already fake-dating, so all my carefully placed boundaries are out the window now.

We pass the food around the table and fill our plates.

"Oh, I almost forgot!" I reach into my jacket pocket and pull out a large bag of Sour Patch Kids and set them on the table.

They're Sophie's favorite. She squeals and reaches for them. "Have I mentioned you're my favorite brother?" she teases.

Drew rolls his eyes.

"Brooks Windell! What is that??" My mother demands.

"You told me I had to bring something since I couldn't help with the cooking."

"*That's* not what I meant." She glares at the bag of candy. "Molly is going to think we're animals!"

Molly laughs. "No, I only think Brooks is an animal." She nudges me with her elbow. "He's the one who introduced me to junk food."

"You're welcome," I tell her. "Molly didn't even know what McDonald's was before she met me. And she hadn't seen *any* good movies. The only reason I stayed friends with her was because she'd at least seen *Ducktales*."

Sophie, who's happily chowing down on the candy and ignoring the food on her plate, starts to giggle and sing the theme song for *Ducktales*. I join in and Molly, Drew, and my parents look at us like we're insane.

"What kind of films did your family enjoy?" Mom asks, leaning over so she can see Molly.

"My parents felt like television should only be used educationally ... So the few times we watched movies, they were in French or Spanish. We were also allowed to watch adaptations of classic literature, such as *Pride and Prejudice* and *Anne of Green Gables*."

"So then how'd you discover *Ducktales*?" Sophie asks, popping another Sour Patch Kid into her mouth. Drew brings a fork full of green beans up to her mouth and she shoos his hand away.

"When my parents traveled or entertained, we'd have a nanny. One of them, Gertrude, was pretty lenient about TV. She'd let us watch it before bed if we promised not to tell." Molly laughs and everyone joins her.

There's a pause in conversation while we eat. Dad takes a sip of wine and clears his throat. "Brooks, how's your knee replacement design coming along?"

Mom narrows her eyes at me. "I thought your work was top secret?"

I grimace and shoot my dad a perturbed look. He mouths the word *sorry*.

"Sorry, Mom. Dad has some good insight for my work sometimes since he's an orthopedic surgeon and all."

She nods, looking appeased for now.

"It's going okay, I just want to make sure it feels like a real knee and not just another knee replacement implant. Vanderwin is still such a new company and we need to stay ahead of the curve."

"True. Well, the Vanderwin breast and glute implants have had great success so far. I'm sure you'll create a ground-breaking design for this, too." He smiles encouragingly.

My mother's phone starts to ring loudly. "Oh! It's David and Isabella FaceTiming. Let me grab the iPad so we can see them better." She jumps up from her seat and dashes into the next room before coming back five seconds later and answering the FaceTime call on the device.

David's surly face comes into view along with Isa's charming smile. Mom is so delighted to see them, her voice is an octave higher than normal. "It's so wonderful to see your faces! We sure wish you were here. The table seems so empty."

"What are we, Mom? Chopped liver?" I ask sarcastically.

I can see David smirking on the screen.

"Yeah, what the hell? At least we gave you grandchildren!" Sophie says to Mom before laughing.

"Language, young lady." Mom shoots her a stern look before smiling back at the iPad screen.

David hums, making a show of narrowing his eyes and looking in the direction of me and Molly. "Umm, Brooks ... that isn't a *date*, is it?"

Molly laughs. "Nope! It's just me!"

My face falls for a moment before I right myself and force out a laugh. "Ha. Yep, just my good pal, Molly."

She bumps her fist on my shoulder playfully, showing David that we're just buddies ... totally platonic ... never picturing each other naked.

At least ... one of us isn't.

"Oh, Molly. Good to see you. Glad you can help fill the table up," David says in his dry, monotone voice.

Molly just laughs again.

"So where are you two now?" Drew asks David and Isa.

Isa grins. "We're in Barcelona! It's so gorgeous."

"Oooh, how romantic!" Sophie says with hearts in her eyes ... not literally, of course. She looks at Drew. "We should go to Barcelona."

He leans in and rubs his nose against hers. "Let's do it."

I make a gagging noise and they glare at me. "We don't want to hear about your *newlywedding*."

"Our what?" Sophie asks, looking confused.

Drew continues glaring at me. "Nothing, sweetie."

I grin back at him before looking over at Molly. She whispers, "What's *newlywedding*?"

Leaning in to whisper in her ear, I respond, "I'll tell you when you're older."

She giggles and shoves me playfully. I don't move right away, loving the rush of being so close to her that my mouth is nearly brushing her earlobe. I can smell her shampoo and her Chanel No. 5 and have to stop myself from sniffing her and nuzzling her neck.

This is the most I've ever enjoyed a family dinner.

Chapter 11

Molly

Seeing Brooks with his family was enlightening. I found myself noting all the differences between Brooks and Todd ... and the differences were startling. I thought quiet, broody men were the whole package. They're so romantic, dramatic, and poised.

But watching my light and cheery best friend rough-house with his nieces and teasing his mother and sister was ... dare I say, attractive?

Of course, I've seen Brooks's charm come out before, especially when he's around women. But seeing his personality in his natural habitat like I did today gave me a weird feeling in my gut. I wouldn't call it butterflies ... maybe it just surprised me that I noticed how attractive he was.

His romantic attention has never been wholly directed on me, and for the first time since asking him to be
my wedding date and faux boyfriend, I'm apprehensive
I might not be able to withstand his charm. That I might
confuse what's real and what's fake ... That I could possibly even discover that my best friend is ... kind of sexy.

Even despite him being bright and cheerful, blonde
and sparkling... not dark and serious at all. What if *my
type* is challenged indefinitely?

Not saying Brooks *is* my type, of course. But just that
... maybe dark and broody isn't my only type, after all?

Brooks pulls to a stop in my driveway. I don't get out
right away, relishing the warm cabin of his truck and the
soothing Christmas music playing on the radio. I glance
at him from my seat and notice his backwards baseball
cap is back on now that his mom can't lecture him about
it.

Brooks's elbow goes to the center console and he
turns toward me, breaking the silence. "So, is everything set for our trip? The office is closed this week
except for Hope checking the messages, right?"

"Yep! We're good to go. Are you ready for this?"

He leans toward me, the light from my front porch
reflecting in his eyes. "Be prepared to have your socks
blown off by my boyfriend performance."

I shake my head like I'm annoyed, but I can't help the laugh that bubbles out of me. "It will be Oscar-worthy, no doubt."

"I'd even settle for a daytime Emmy." He winks. "I'll pick you up early Tuesday morning?"

I nod. "I expect you to be bright-eyed and bushy-tailed. Are you sure you can manage a six a.m. wake up and still be able to drive us to the airport?" I know how much he hates waking up early.

"Maybe I should hire a car to drive us." He gives me a boyish grin. "That's probably what you're used to. Would a Rolls-Royce suffice?"

I wrinkle my nose as if put off by a Rolls-Royce. "Hm, I guess it'll work this once. I usually prefer a Mercedes-Benz though."

He throws his head back and laughs, making his thick, muscular throat visible. I've never noticed a man's throat before … Maybe because Todd's wasn't a good one?

Does my noticing Brooks's throat make *his* a good one? If it wasn't then I probably wouldn't have noticed it. Perhaps it's the throat muscles that draw all the females' attention to my best friend.

Feeling flustered by where my thoughts have landed me, I unbuckle my seatbelt. "Okay, well … See you Tuesday. Thanks for taking me out tonight. Your family is awesome."

He hesitates for the briefest moment, making me wonder what's going through his mind. "You're always welcome, Molly."

I open the truck door and slide out before walking quickly to my front door and unlocking it. Brooks, of course, doesn't leave until he sees that I'm safely inside my house. I'm glued to the small window at my front door, watching his truck drive off and wondering why I can't seem to look away.

Early Tuesday morning, Brooks arrives to pick me up. It's so early, the sun has barely begun rising over the horizon. In other words, way too early for Brooks Windell. I stifle a laugh when I open my front door and see him standing there, all groggy and adorable, with his hair tousled. He's wearing a hoodie and jeans, and a sleepy expression. Luckily for him, he can pull off the casual, just-rolled-out-of-bed look better than anyone I know.

"Good morning, sleepyhead!" I greet him then turn and reach for my luggage.

Brooks rushes forward, well, as fast as he rushes this early in the morning. "Hands off—let me get that. What kind of lousy fake boyfriend do you think I am?" he teases, taking the suitcase from me and picking it up to carry it down the porch steps. I can tell it's easy for him to lift, but he groans dramatically, nevertheless. "Geez, woman! How long are you planning on being gone?"

"We've been friends for six years, and you're going to act surprised that I'm not a light packer?"

"True."

I harumph, but his smirk tells me he knows I'm being sarcastic. "Be right back!" I say. "I made us lattes."

"Praise the Lord!" he yells up toward the sky.

I duck back inside and grab the lattes from my entry-way table, locking the door and pulling it closed behind me with my foot. I walk towards Brooks's truck, where Brooks is currently lifting my luggage into the backseat. He's still pretending that my suitcase is too heavy for him, putting on quite a show with lots of groaning and complaining.

I extend a latte toward him, and he takes it with a sleepy smile, forgetting how heavy my luggage apparently was.

He closes his eyes and sniffs the steam coming from the travel lid. "Mmm. Smells like heaven."

"It's a pecan maple latte," I tell him proudly.

Brooks opens the passenger door for me before saying, "Maple? Getting us in the mood for Vermont, eh?"

"You know they don't have Canadian accents in Vermont, right?"

He chuckles, waiting until I'm seated before shutting my door for me. I watch him run around the vehicle to the driver's side. The air is so cold this morning I can see his breath as he runs. Brooks is the only person I know who would be perfectly content just wearing a hoodie when it's this cold outside. But the man's temperature does always seem to run 10 degrees hotter than everyone else's.

When he gets inside, he puts his cup in the cup holder and blasts the heater as high as it will go, then faces all the vents in my direction. "So, you're telling me they don't cut their food with hockey skates up there and drink maple syrup like it's water?"

He puts his hand on my headrest and cranes his head around to back out of my driveway. Weirdly, I notice the muscles in his neck again. Since I've met Brooks, I haven't once noticed his neck until now ... Has he been working out his neck muscles or something?

"Under normal circumstances, I would encourage you to drag some old skates to the dinner table and try cutting your food. It would make a hilarious show, and the horrified looks on my parents' faces would give me something to laugh about for years to come ..."

He side-eyes me before returning his gaze to the busy highway as he drives. "I'm sensing a *but*."

"*But* ... I'm gonna need you to be on your best behavior. I'm talking Diane Windell-level expectations."

He whines, "What? Nooooo."

"The point of this whole charade is to avoid my family pushing me to get back together with Todd. If they think my new lover is some uncultured yeti man, they'll never leave me alone."

He gasps. "Yeti man? I'm offended." He laughs and looks at me again. "Your parents already know I went to MIT and own a successful business—with their daughter. So how badly could they possibly think of me?"

I whistle a breath out slowly. "You obviously don't know my parents very well. They're total snobs, Brooks."

He grins. "If I remember correctly ... a certain someone I know was pretty stuck up when I first met her."

I laugh. He's not wrong. "I know, I know. But thankfully a down-to-earth Kansas boy showed me a different way of life."

"Slumming it with a millionaire," he says with grandeur, moving one hand from left to right in front of his face like it's a movie title.

"New reality show?" I ask, and we both laugh.

We make it to the airport, check our bags, and find our gate. I've never flown with Brooks before, but the man is the center of attention everywhere he goes. Without even trying. I don't know whether to be annoyed or impressed. I'm pretty sure the TSA lady selected him for a random pat down just so she could feel him up.

Now the woman seated next to us has been flirting with him for ten minutes. She doesn't even seem to notice me.

Todd and I did a fair amount of traveling together, and, of course, women would glance at him appreciatively. But the attention Brooks gets is on an entirely different level. You'd think he was a celebrity.

The bubbly blonde woman next to Brooks must be starting to annoy him, too, because he leans back in his chair and drapes an arm around the back of mine. The woman looks between us curiously then continues chatting and ignoring me.

Brooks interrupts her and turns to me. "Do you need me to get you anything before our flight boards, muffin butt?"

Muffin butt? Out of all the pet names he could've used. I look at him adoringly. "I'm good, boogie-bear. But thanks for the offer."

Miss Flirty-pants laughs awkwardly. "I think I'll grab a drink before our flight leaves. Nice chatting with you."

Brooks nods and she scurries off toward the gift shop.

"I didn't think she'd ever shut up. If I had to hear about her three cats for one more second I was going to lose my mind." He drags one hand through his hair, making it look messier and somehow even better than it already did.

I roll my lips together to keep from laughing.

"Don't laugh!" he says in an offended tone. "It's your job as my fake girlfriend to bat all the other girls away from me."

"Not if you keep calling me *muffin butt!*" I whisper-yell.

He laughs. "I thought you'd like that."

"Where did you even come up with that? It's awful!"

He shrugs. "Well, the man over there is eating a muffin ... and you kind of have a good butt. So it just slipped out."

I blink a few times, surprised. "I have a good butt?"

He wiggles uncomfortably in his seat, and I have the inkling he hadn't meant to say that out loud. He clears his throat. "Objectively speaking ... as a straight male ... yes."

"Huh," I say, still baffled. "Todd never mentioned my butt."

Brooks's head whips over to look at me directly. "Are you serious?"

Now I'm the one feeling uncomfortable. This is territory Brooks and I have never entered in our friendship. We don't talk in detail about the people we date, and we definitely don't talk about each other's derrieres.

"Yeah ... but I mean, he complimented other things."

He scoffs. "What, like your mind?"

My jaw drops and I smack his shoulder. "Yes, in fact! What's wrong with that?"

He crosses his arms over his chest with a smug smile on his face. "Nothing. It's just ... Most women already know they have a great mind. What they *don't* know is if they have a good butt."

I shake my head but can't help but laugh at his words. "Well ... you're not wrong."

Ten minutes later, our flight boards. We're in first class and the flight attendant brings us complimentary champagne. Of course, both flight attendants happen to be young and female ... and instantly enamored with Brooks.

"Can I get you anything else, sir? Anything at all?" The brunette one bats her lashes at him.

"We're good." He places his hand on top of mine. "But thank you."

She gives me a tight smile then walks to her seat at the front of the plane.

I start laughing to myself and Brooks eyes me curiously. "What's so funny?"

"How do you deal with this all the time?"

He furrows his brow. "Deal with what?"

I lower my voice to a whisper. "Having the attention of every female under the age of seventy-five on you at all times."

His head jerks back as if he's offended. "That is not true." He pauses. "I also have the attention of the ones *over* seventy-five."

"Oh, you're so full of it!" I give him a playful push and he throws his head back laughing like he does when he really thinks something is funny.

I turn to face the window to keep myself from looking at his neck.

Chapter 12

Brooks

Junior Year MIT

"Hey, what are you doing tonight? Wanna watch a movie?" I ask Molly after studying together for our exam. It's Friday night, and I've already had several girls ask me out. But all I really want to do is hang out with Molly Vanderbilt.

She smiles. "Actually, Todd is taking me to a new restaurant. The Zagat Guide says it's amazing."

My heart plummets inside my chest at the idea of her spending the evening with Todd. Will she hold his hand across the table? Allow him to stare into her big blue eyes? Or even slide her hands into his hair when he kisses her?

I give my head a subtle shake and try to think of something else. *Anything* else.

"Didn't Britt ask you out after class this morning? You should take her to a movie! She's probably way more fun than me anyway," Molly says with a light-hearted chuckle.

Impossible.

"Yeah." I force a laugh. "She's hot. I should call her."

Molly rolls her eyes but her expression is amused. "Is that pretty much your only prerequisite for a girl?"

"No," I say defensively. I want to say more but stop myself.

I want to tell her my prerequisites are sparkly blue eyes that are like looking straight into a sapphire, a heart-shaped face framed by dark hair with cute bangs, a body dressed like a modern version of an old lady, and extra points for an antique spoon collection being her prized possession.

She tilts her head forward, waiting for me to go on. "So? What are they!"

"Hot *and* desperate," I tease.

She bursts into laughter and shoves me with her dainty hands. "You scandalous rake! I can't wait to meet the girl who reforms you into a gentleman someday."

If only she realized the only girl I can picture marrying is sitting right in front of me.

"Oh! My father sent me some new dresses. Help me choose one."

I gulp, knowing this is way out of my depth and I think Molly would look sexy in a gunny sack. "Yeah, sure."

She jumps up from her seat on the bed and strolls to her closet. She rifles through the clothing before pulling out a pale blue skirt and jacket combo and a little black dress with tiny straps to hold up the top.

"The blue one," I say quickly, not wanting anyone, except for myself, to see Molly in that little black dress.

"Really?" she asks, looking between the two dresses. "I just knew you'd say the black one."

I shrug. "The blue has that understated class that's kind of your signature."

Her eyes widen and she smiles. "Brooks, that's so sweet!"

She walks toward me and my breath hitches when she stands on her toes and puckers her lips slightly. I'm very aware of the way my heart is racing at her close proximity ... but then my heart rate plummets when her lips land briefly, very briefly, on my cheek.

"You're the best friend a girl could ask for," she says with a genuine smile before patting me on the arm and hanging the black dress back inside her closet. She glances over at the clock next to her bed. "Oh! I better start getting ready. See you Monday at class!"

Molly spins on her heel and takes her outfit into the bathroom with her. Knowing a dismissal when I see one, I let myself out of her dorm room and begrudgingly pull out my phone.

Maybe Britt will be the one to make me forget Molly?

Chapter 13

Brooks

After landing in Vermont, I guffaw with laughter when a Mercedes-Benz pulls up to get us from the airport.

Molly sighs. "Don't even start."

A man in a suit, who looks like a modern version of a butler, gets out and takes Molly's bag and then mine. "Miss Vanderbilt, Mr. Windell. I trust your flight was comfortable?"

"Yes, very much so. Thank you, Harold."

I open the door for Molly, and she slides into the back seat. I get in beside her and quickly, before Harold finishes putting our bags in the trunk, I whisper, "I trust your flight was comfortable??" I snicker. "Should I ask him if his mother is in good health?"

She giggles, then brings her index finger to her lips, gesturing for me to be quiet. "Shh! He'll hear you."

Harold slides into the front seat and checks his mirrors before pulling out into the airport traffic.

"Your parents are thrilled to see you, ma'am," Harold says in a monotone voice, void of any emotion.

"I'll be glad to see them as well," she replies with a polite smile.

I glance at her from the side and she gives me a subtle shake of her head. A silent plea not to ask about her parents in Harold's company, perhaps?

We drive through the rolling hills of Vermont and arrive at a long winding driveway. Gold gates with lions on each side open slowly after Harold punches in the gate code.

Raising my eyebrows, I smirk at Molly. She shakes her head in dismay, but looks amused.

The posh mansion comes into view after we make it past the snow-covered evergreen trees that line the first quarter mile of the driveway.

"Umm ... I thought you said it was a cabin?" I ask, my jaw dropping as I take in the giant house before me.

"It *is* a cabin," Molly insists.

Harold silently gets out of the car and walks around to get our bags from the trunk.

"This is not a cabin!" I whisper-yell, looking back to make sure Harold is distracted. "I'm pretty sure this is where one of the Kardashians live."

Molly waves a hand in the air like this house isn't that big of a deal. But I see the beginnings of a blush on her face before she turns away from me. She opens her door and slides out of the car before Harold or I can do it for her.

I get out on my side and rush around the Mercedes-Benz, careful not to slip in the snow. When I make it to her side, I gently grab her arm. "Hey, what's wrong?"

She leans in and whispers, "Don't pretend like you've never seen a mansion, Brooks. You're *also* from a wealthy family."

My head jerks back slightly at her clipped tone. I remind myself to tone the teasing down. I'm here to make her life easier, not more difficult. "Sorry. I know it's annoying when people react like that. This is just even more grand than I ever expected."

She sighs, and her expression softens. "I know. I'm sorry for being grumpy ... it's just that my family makes me feel on edge. And just because it's a giant house doesn't mean it's better somehow than other houses. Your parents' house is so warm and gorgeous. It may be smaller than this ... but your family is loving. They genuinely enjoy being around each other." She looks behind her and lowers her voice as if someone might hear us talking. "The Vanderbilts aren't like that."

Unsure what to say, I take her hand in mine. She hasn't put gloves on since we're not planning on staying outside long. Molly looks up at me in surprise.

"You said unlimited hand holding," I remind her.

She chuckles. "Oh, right. I suppose we might as well get used to it. My family could see us anytime now." She tugs on my hand to pull me toward the grand staircase leading up to the gigantic front door.

I'm pretty sure they chopped down a five-hun-dred-year-old tree to create this door. Molly grabs the gold knocker and knocks twice before the door opens and we're greeted by another man who looks like a butler.

I'm briefly surprised that not only does she have to knock before entering a cabin owned by her own flesh and blood, but also her parents aren't the ones to greet us. I look over at Molly to see if she's upset, but she looks unfazed.

"Miss Vanderbilt, welcome home," the butler says in the same monotone voice as Harold.

We step inside the foyer, complete with glossy, tile floors—tile that's been made to look like wood grain. I'm guessing the tile is heated. The inside does look like a cabin, but like it's been staged. Not the type of cabin where you'd spend the day outdoors to come in and throw off your wet snow clothes and cozy up by the fire... but like a cabin where a home decor magazine photo shoot had just taken place.

I've been so busy studying the interior of the cabin, I hadn't noticed Molly had already shrugged her coat off and the butler is looking at me expectantly.

"Oh! So sorry." I take my hoodie off and hand it to him.

"Thank you, sir," he says dryly before walking off down a long hallway with Molly's coat draped over one arm, and holding my hoodie between his thumb and forefinger like it's a diseased animal.

I grimace at Molly and she laughs quietly.

She studies me for a moment, brings her hand up and smooths my hair down, then dusts a piece of lint off my dark-green, long-sleeved henley. "There. Now you're ready."

She slides her hand into mine and I follow her lead through the entryway and into a room with ceilings so high you could store the Titanic inside. There are stairs going up on both sides and then meeting in the middle to a balcony.

An attractive couple that I recognize as Molly's parents begin walking—no, more like gliding, down the staircase. It's like they've been waiting up there for us to walk in so they could make their regal entrance.

Mr. Vanderbilt, who has the same dark hair as Molly, is wearing black tailored trousers and a white dress shirt. Mrs. Vanderbilt complements him perfectly with her blonde, perfectly coiffed hair and fitted black dress.

"Mary Elizabeth, how wonderful to see you," her mother says as she finally reaches us. It feels like we watched them walk down those stairs for five minutes. "And we're honored you brought your friend with you." She smiles politely at me, but there's something in her eyes that seems annoyed at my presence. She gives Molly a pat on the shoulder that's awkward, like she forced herself to show affection to look more human or something.

Her father shakes my hand firmly. "Mr. Windell, pleasure seeing you again." He then kisses Molly on top of the head. "Darling, so glad you're here."

Molly's sister appears at the top of the opposite stairway with a man at her side who I assume is her fiancé. She scurries past him, a big smile on her face. I notice her mother gives her a sharp look and she slows her steps on the stairs to appease her.

"Molly!" Mildred exclaims, looking genuinely happy to see her sister. Her fiancé finally catches up to her and they hug Molly before turning their attention to me. Mildred looks me up and down before saying, "Yes, you'll do very nicely."

I quirk a brow and she just smirks at me.

"I'm Preston, Mildred's fiancé," the dark-haired man, who slightly resembles Todd, holds out his hand. His look isn't harsh or angry, but also not overly friendly. His expression almost reminds me of an apprehensive puppy who will be chastised if he's too friendly.

I shake his hand. "I'm Brooks. Thanks for allowing me to attend. I'm thrilled to be Molly's date." I wrap an arm around her waist and pull her closer to me. She brings her hand up to rest on my chest and smiles at me.

My cotton tee isn't very thick and I swear I feel Molly's fingers cupping my pec ever so slightly. It's probably all in my head, but I flex my chest—just in case.

Mrs. Vanderbilt clears her throat. "Well, why don't we show you to your room so you can both get settled?"

I notice she said *room*, as in one. But Molly assured me we'd have our own rooms. Molly loops her arm through mine as we trudge up what feels like one-thousand steps.

Her mother leads us to a large room that's immaculately staged and decorated just like the rest of the house seems to be. There's a queen size sleigh bed with navy blue bedding that's covered with decorative throw pillows. A large wooden door is ajar, leading to a bathroom, and my and Molly's luggage is at the foot of the bed.

I glance at Molly and raise an eyebrow. She looks just as shocked as I feel and laughs nervously. "Uh, Mother ... where is Brooks staying?"

Mrs. Vanderbilt purses her lips. "Oh, I know we've always insisted on separate rooms for unmarried couples, but there simply isn't enough room this time with all the guests arriving Thursday. Every room is spoken for. And since I assumed Todd would be your date ... I hadn't considered it would be a big deal."

Molly glances at me once more, looking pale. "I promised Brooks he'd have his own room."

Mrs. Vanderbilt looks down at her diamond encrusted wristwatch and heaves an annoyed sigh before looking directly at me. "Brooks, do you really mind sharing a room with my beautiful daughter? Are you Amish or something?"

"Mother!" Molly gasps. "He doesn't have to be Amish to want privacy."

"You're both adults, sweetheart. Let's not be coy."

Molly looks upset. Her nostrils are flared and her arms are crossed over her chest. Before she can speak, I place my hand on her back and give her mother my most charming smile. "This room will be just perfect. Thank you, Mrs. Vanderbilt." I turn to Molly, who's looking at me like I've lost my mind. "Don't worry, sugar lips; this will allow us to spend even more time together."

The corner of her mouth twitches, and her eyes glitter with amusement. She uncrosses her arms and leans into me with a sigh. "I suppose you're right, hunky bear."

Mrs. Vanderbilt sniffs haughtily at our pet names, but looks slightly relieved she doesn't have to scrounge up another room for me at the last minute. "Wonderful. I'll let you two get settled. Dinner will be served promptly at seven."

She leaves us and we both stare silently at the bed.

Chapter 14

Molly

"Sooo," Brooks says, not making eye contact. "I could sleep on the floor?"

I breathe in a deep breath through my nose, attempting to calm my racing heart. "You're not sleeping on the floor. The bed is plenty big enough for us both. It'll be like a sleepover!" I try to sound excited, but my voice is coming out super high and squeaky.

He finally looks at me. "Molly, it's a queen size bed. I'm not exactly a small man."

I look down at his feet, which are big. Then my eyes travel up his long legs, stopping briefly where his quad muscles strain against his dark jeans, then continuing up to his chest—which I now know is quite firm—then his broad shoulders. Next is his neck, which I just recently noticed. His Adam's apple bobs like my stare is making him uncomfortable. My eyes glide to his chiseled jaw, another male feature that's greatly overlooked. A strong jaw connected to a thick muscled neck? Totally swoon worthy.

He has to be almost a foot taller than I am, not to mention eighty pounds heavier.

Finally, I meet his gaze and wrinkle my nose. "Yeah, you're bigger than I realized ... you'll probably take up most of the bed."

He smirks. "There are enough throw pillows to create a whole separate bed on the floor."

"No. It's seriously fine. You're some kind of Swedish giant, but *I'm* tiny. Miniscule. I'll take up like this much room." I hold my hands about twelve inches apart.

"Well, we can decide after dinner." He looks at me skeptically. "Do you need the bathroom? I was going to take a quick shower before we head downstairs."

The room suddenly seems too warm. Am I blushing? I feel like I'm blushing. And there goes my sweat mustache again.

Brooks is just going to be right through that door, completely naked? This situation is way more of a test of our friendship than I thought it would be. Especially with sharing a bedroom *and* a bathroom.

"No, go ahead!" My voice sounds squeaky again. "I'll just use the vanity to touch up my makeup."

"All right." He shrugs and grabs his suitcase, hoisting it onto the bench at the foot of the bed. He unzips it and pulls out a leather toiletry bag, then slips off his shoes and socks and walks to the bathroom.

When I hear the click of the door closing behind him, I grab my own suitcase and rummage through it to find my makeup bag. I sit at the vanity and begin powdering my face when I notice the tinge of pink on my cheeks. I glare at my reflection.

"Brooks is your best friend. It's completely normal for friends to have sleepovers. Stop making it weird," I whisper to myself before taking a deep breath and continue readying myself for dinner.

I walk to the walk-in closet, knowing my mother will have stocked it with designer clothing. Clothing that will be labeled for each event and expected to be worn as such. Sure enough, there's a long-sleeved, green cocktail dress with a label tied to the hanger. The label reads, *Calvin Klein. Dinner Tuesday evening.* I spin the hanger and notice the dress is backless except for a tie at the neck. I won't be able to wear a bra with it, but thankfully the fabric is thick enough that it won't be a big deal. Sometimes it's nice not being well-endowed up top.

If I didn't love the gorgeous velvet dress so much, I might have put up a fight. Actually, that's not true. My greatest strength is making everyone around me at ease and bringing peace into every situation ... but it's also my greatest weakness. Standing up for what I want has always been a struggle.

Peeking out of the closet, I make sure the shower is still running and quickly remove my travel clothes, slip the dress on, and tie the ribbon at the back of the neck. Next, I select some gold strappy heels and fasten them around my ankles. I do a spin in front of the full-length mirror and smile. If my mother is going to pick out my clothes for me like I'm an incompetent three-year-old who might show up in rainbow tights, rubber boots and tie dye t-shirt, at least she has good taste.

I walk out of the closet at the same time Brooks walks out of the bathroom, leaving us only a few feet from each other. My eyes widen at the sight of him in nothing but a towel, and I gasp before I can stop myself.

"Sorry, I forgot to grab my clothes out of my suitcase," he says quickly, walking to his open suitcase, taking out some clothes, then heading back towards the bathroom door. AKA right next to me.

I barely hear him as I take in his naked, glistening torso. His entire top half ripples with every movement he makes, showing his defined muscles. Muscles that are still wet from his shower.

Finally, my brain starts to work again and I clamp my mouth shut and shrug my shoulders. "No big deal, bestie!" I lean toward him and pat his glistening chest—in an effort to seem chill and neutral to his muscled physique. I mean, he isn't even my type. I'm attracted to dark, slim, poetic types. But as a biomedical engineer, I can appreciate the human body and what a work of art it can be. Plus, the man I'm in business with has obviously worked very hard at the gym. Good for him! What better quality in a business partner than hardworking?

I wonder what exercises result in that very defined V-shape he has going on below his abdominals. The human body is *so* fascinating. Scientifically speaking, of course.

One side of his mouth quirks up, like he can't decide whether to be amused by my chest pat or freaked out by it. "Okay," he says slowly before he smiles for real, noticing my outfit. "Wow, you look gorgeous."

"Oh, thanks." I shrug again. My shoulders are going to get as big as Brooks's with all the shrugging I've been doing.

He turns back toward the bathroom and closes the door behind him again. I must've started holding my breath after the shoulder shrug because as soon as he's out of sight, I exhale a deep breath like I've been underwater for a full minute.

"Stop looking so annoyed," Brooks whispers, grabbing my hand in his as we walk down the staircase to the dining room. "You told me to blend in and not draw attention."

I close my eyes and take a deep, steadying breath. "And that's what you thought would blend in?" I say, looking directly at his hideous bow tie.

With his free hand, he adjusts the navy-blue bow tie that has a corgi pattern on it. Yes, corgis. Tiny corgis are embroidered all over it. "Rich people love corgis!" he insists. "*And* bow ties!"

"I knew I should've hired a professional male escort."

He gasps dramatically. "That hurts, Molly."

I turn to look at him, narrowing my eyes when I see the mischievous expression on his face. "Kind of like your tie is hurting my eyes?"

He looks down at his tie ... and talks to it. "Don't let her hurt you, little guys. Even the queen loved you." He looks up at the ceiling and closes his eyes in reverence. "God rest her soul."

I tap my foot on the marble step and keep my eyes narrowed on him.

"Do you want me to change?" he asks, finally taking me seriously.

"No! Then we'll be late. And that will draw even more attention."

He nods, looking abashed. "After tonight, I won't wear any more corgi stuff. But ..." He trails off with a smirk on his face.

"But what?"

"I have a Highland cow bowtie that's really classy."

I quirk my head to the side and keep my face stoic, even though I kind of want to laugh. How could a tie with a cow on it possibly be classy? "How about no animal clothing?"

He heaves a heavy sigh, looking genuinely disappointed. "Okay, you're the boss."

I laugh. "Why don't you save your new animal outfits for when we're back home? I really want to see that tie."

He grins, and I'm glad to see the look of disappointment disappear. "You'll love it. He looks just like Cowlvin," he says, referencing the Highland cow painting I gave him.

We laugh together as we continue into the formal dining room, which kind of looks like Gaston's hunting den from *Beauty and the Beast*. Deer antler chandeliers line the ceiling and everything is fur and leather ... even though no one in my family hunts.

We're still snickering when we discover everyone is already seated at the table. The room is very quiet, and now everyone is staring at us.

"Care to enlighten us on what's so amusing?" my father asks from the head of the table, his fingers steepled.

My mother glances at her fancy wristwatch. "You're late."

Mildred looks at me with a sympathetic smile, widening her eyes as if silently saying our parents are ridiculous. I look at the huge wooden clock above the fireplace at the front of the room. Sure enough, we're one minute late.

Brooks places one hand at the small of my back, a small but comforting gesture. His hand feels warm as it brushes the bare skin on my lower back. "Sorry, Mr. and Mrs. Vanderbilt. It was completely my fault. My hair just wouldn't cooperate."

Everyone at the table chuckles at his joke and we take our seats across from Preston and Mildred. I'm relieved that it's just my family here along with Brooks and Preston. I wasn't sure if Todd and Trudy would arrive today.

The moment our backsides hit the padded leather chairs, a myriad of servers appear with silver trays. They serve us silently and then leave back through the door they came in from. Brooks eyes me from the side, his expression strained. I can tell he's trying so hard not to laugh at the fanfare.

I widen my eyes as a silent plea for him to just leave it be and eat.

Unable to help himself, he lifts his water glass to his mouth ... his pinky out the entire time.

Chapter 15

Brooks

O kay, Molly's family is faaaaancy. Like way fancy. No wonder she doesn't bring anyone around them. The Vanderbilts are practically dripping with pretension and snobbery. Never in my life have I felt poor until arriving here this afternoon.

Throughout my life, I've had plenty of people want to be my friend because of my family's influence or wealth. Hell, half the women I've taken on dates have only wanted me for those things. But here at the Vanderbilt's? I'm just a pauper.

The meal smells and looks incredible. I'm about to dig into my filet mignon when I look around and realize everyone else is just picking at their food.

Molly glances at me and must notice my trepidation. She whispers, "Just go ahead and eat. My family serves meals for show ... they'll all have a diet protein shake after this."

I snicker as I cut into my steak and take a large bite. I withhold a moan as the meat melts in my mouth. It's perfect. I swallow and cut off another bite. "This is amazing."

Molly's parents watch me dig into my food with barely disguised disgust on their faces. Molly finally starts eating her meal too while everyone else simply picks at their salads. Preston watches each bite I take closely, looking like he might drool.

When I finish my meal, I lean towards Molly. "So, are they gonna finish theirs? Because I could still eat."

She snorts, drawing a glare from her mother. "Your appetite never ceases to amaze me."

I flex my arm while bringing a fork full of salad to my mouth. She subtly shakes her head at my antics and I wink at her. "Gotta get my nutrition in for these gains."

"Are those ..." Mildred's voice draws my attention from across the table. Her eyes are squinting in the direction of my neck. "Corgis?"

Puffing my chest out with pride, I answer, "Yes they are corgis. Thank you."

One of her perfectly shaped eyebrows goes up. "It wasn't a compliment."

Preston chokes on the sip of water he just drank.

"Mildred Annelise. Manners, please," Mrs. Vandervbilt reprimands her then daintily dabs her mouth with her cloth napkin although I have no idea why, since she hasn't even eaten anything.

Mr. Vanderbilt rests his elbows on the table and rubs his temples with his index fingers before groaning. "Can we just have one nice family dinner without all this ruckus?"

I look at Molly. "What ruckus?" I whisper.

She widens her eyes, which I think is Vanderbilt for *shut up*.

The side door opens and the servers enter the room again with more silver trays. They place a slice of tiramisu in front of each of us then take everyone's dinner plates and exit silently.

I watch them leave, slack-jawed that they didn't even let these people finish their meal.

Molly clears her throat from the seat next to me. "You're gaping."

I snap my jaw shut. "Sorry."

Why even serve dessert when they're not going to eat it? What a tragic waste of good filet mignon and tiramisu. I wonder if I could sneak into the kitchen trash tonight. My mother would be appalled at the thought.

Devouring my dessert without another thought, I keep glancing around the room to see if anyone else is eating. Molly is taking small bites, but is almost done with hers. Good girl.

Mildred swiped her slim finger through the cocoa powder on top and then licked it off with a contented sigh. Preston took two bites and now looks like an ashamed child that ate a cookie before dinner. Mrs. Vanderbilt sniffed hers and smiled. Like sniffing it was good enough for her. Mr. Vanderbilt took one bite and went back to looking stressed out.

It's like I'm reading *The Very Hungry Caterpillar* in reverse. And without the fun illustrations.

After what feels like an eternity—but was maybe twenty minutes?—dessert is taken away as silently as it was served. My plate is the only empty one. It was so good I could've licked the plate clean, but I refrained.

"We're pretty tired from traveling today. May we be excused?" Molly asks, directing the question to her parents.

"Of course, get some sleep tonight," Her father tells her before narrowing his eyes on me.

I experience a brief moment of confusion until I realize he thinks I'm *sleeping* with his daughter. Well, at least our ruse is working? I smile back at him. This is fun.

Molly leads the way out of the dining room and into the quiet hallway that leads to the stairs. I follow her and she releases a heavy sigh, her shoulders relaxing for the first time since we arrived here. I place my hands on her shoulders from behind her and give them a quick rub.

She laughs and shoos my hands away. "No one is even watching us right now!"

"You never know when someone might be watching," I point to a security camera on the ceiling.

Molly rolls her eyes. "Hey, did you bring your swimsuit?"

"No. But I'm always up for skinny dipping."

She whips around to look at me and I laugh. "Yes, I brought a swimsuit. Calm down."

She breathes a sigh of relief. "Whew. I'm not sure our friendship could handle sharing a bed *and* skinny dipping."

I chuckle to keep things playful, but I honestly can't think of anything better than the two things she just mentioned.

When we arrive back at our room, we open our suitcases and pull our swimsuits out. Before ducking into the bathroom to change into her suit, Molly says, "Hey, the hot tub is right out on our balcony, so you can head out there once you've changed."

"We have a balcony??" I gasp. "*With* a hot tub?"

She cocks her head to the side. "Does that honestly surprise you at this point?"

I nod my head at her point. "Yeah … true."

She smirks and closes the bathroom door. I pull my clothes off and slide my trunks on before neatly folding my clothes and putting them away in the dresser across the room. When I walk over toward the French doors that lead to the balcony, I brace myself for the cold air hitting my bare chest. The air is freezing, but I'm pleasantly surprised when my feet hit the heated deck. I should've known.

There's an outdoor fireplace on the large deck and it's already lit as if the staff expected we'd come out here after dinner. Walking over to the luxurious hot tub, I place my phone on the side table and slide into the hot bubbly water. It's heaven.

I sigh and close my eyes, feeling relaxed after that strange dinner. When my phone pings several times in a row, I reluctantly open my eyes and reach for it. I groan when I see a bunch of new messages from my family's group text.

Windell Family Group Chat:

Mom: Brooks, what are you doing in Vermont?

My eyes widen and I swear under my breath. I completely forgot to disable my location on the Find My Friends app.

Sophie: Vermont? Isn't that where Molly's sister's wedding is?

David: You better not be there with a woman.

Madden: #GardenParty #BirthdaySuit

Brooks: Relax. I'm meeting a business client out here. A *male* business client. And Mom, you really need to stay off that stalker app.

Dad: So you're meeting a business client in the same location as the wedding Molly is attending?

"You look serious." Molly's voice surprises me, and I nearly drop my phone into the hot tub.

Looking up, I take in her simple black one piece. It's not a skimpy bikini, but just as tempting. It's like a tease ... an appetizer. Great, now I'm hungry. One filet mignon was *not* enough.

"Ha, yeah. Find my friends ... family chat," I stumble over my words until I look down at my phone again and steady myself.

She slips into the hot tub across from me and I notice she's carrying two stemless wine glasses already full of what looks like wine. I avert my eyes before I start ogling her body again, but look back up when I know she's submerged in water and I can think clearly.

"Is everything okay?" she asks, looking at me with genuine concern and handing me one of the glasses.

I blow out a frustrated breath as I take the glass from her. "Yeah, I just forgot to turn off my location on my mom's stalker app and now the entire family wants to know what the hell I'm doing in Vermont."

Molly grimaces. "Oof. And I think I told Drew and Sophie my sister's wedding is in Vermont?"

"Yep." I shoot her a tight smile and take a sip of the Pinot Grigio. "But this is my fault; don't worry about it. I told them I have a business trip out here."

She looks at me over the brim of her wine glass, which is already half gone. "Seriously? That's the best you could do? Give me your phone."

I shrug and hand her my phone. It's not like this can get any worse. Sipping some more wine, I relax and watch Molly. She bites her bottom lip in concentration, her tongue peeking out as she types a rather long explanation of my location in my family group chat. In an effort to ignore the way her tongue wets her bottom lip while she types, I look at the screen over her shoulder and read what she's writing.

Brooks: Well, when this client wanted to meet in Vermont, we were able to plan the business meeting to coincide with her sister's wedding. Two birds ... one stone. Her family has even been kind enough to allow me to stay with them in one of their guest rooms. I'll fly back home tomorrow night, and Molly will stay for her sister's wedding.

"Not too shabby, Vanderbilt," I tell her, nodding my head with pride.

She bows her head. "Thank you, thank you very much," she says in an Elvis voice.

"An ode to the king of rock. I've never been so proud." I clutch my chest where my heart rests and pretend to shed a tear.

She giggles. "Yeah, you've thoroughly ruined me. My mother would be offended if she knew I listened to anything besides classical music."

"Like Post Malone?" I tease, rolling my lips together in an effort to hide my grin.

She pushes her free hand through the water to splash me, and I laugh heartily. "You were supposed to pretend like you never saw that!"

I splash her back and she gasps then yells, "Stop! You're going to ruin my wine!"

"So, I probably shouldn't mention the nightie either?" I waggle my eyebrows. "That's not what you're wearing tonight is it?" My voice is teasing, but I actually really want to know. Because if that's how she sleeps, I'm definitely making a pallet on the floor. I told myself I would never mention that sexy nightgown ... the wine must be getting to me already. I set the glass down on the side table to avoid getting even more loose with my words.

Molly gasps. "Brooks Windell! You did not just reference my nightgown! And no, that's not what I'll be sleeping in tonight."

Relief washes over me ... paired with a pinch of disappointment. Let's be honest: I'd be crazy to not want to see her in that little nightie again. I'm a hot-blooded man and all that.

Steak.

Beer.

Hunting.

Silky nightgowns.

I laugh again and she rolls her eyes. "You're horrible. Why do women even like you?"

Standing from the water, I give her my best bodybuilder poses. She attempts to act annoyed but I can tell she's trying not to laugh.

"This is how," I say while flexing and posing.

We laugh again, and I'm happy things are normal and not awkward between us. Thank goodness this fake dating nonsense hasn't ruined the best thing in my life ... which is my relationship with Molly. Not to mention we own a business together... Neither of us can just quit if things get weird.

"Speaking of you and women ..." she trails off for a second. "How's your dating ban going?"

I take a deep breath. "Honestly? Not that bad. I've never dated anyone seriously, and it gets old going on dates with women that are just ... meh."

"Meh?" She sounds shocked. "I've seen the women you date, Brooks. They're way more than just *meh*."

"I mean, in looks, sure." I scoff. "This might be difficult for you to believe ..." I gesture at the opulence surrounding us. "But most of them just want to date me because they know my family has money."

She wrinkles her nose and takes another small sip of her wine, which is almost gone now. "Yes, that would get old. I think that's one reason I stayed with Todd so long ... His family is also wealthy, so it wasn't awkward or weird. I knew he didn't want to date me because of my family." She considers her words. "Well, other than the fact our parents are good friends."

I nod once. "That makes sense. But I still think he's a twat waffle."

Chapter 16

Molly

"So, tell me," I say before draining my last drop of wine. "How do you woo all these gorgeous women? Besides the Windell cheek bones."

He huffs out a laugh. "Should I be offended that it's so difficult for you to see why women like me?"

I scoff. "Come on. Give me your best smolder."

His eyes narrow on me, and I suddenly regret drinking that entire glass of wine. He shakes his head slowly from side to side. "Nope. Not going there."

"Please!" I beg. "You'll have to smolder at me eventually anyway, for our ruse."

He scoots away from me. "No way."

"Why not?" I ask, already knowing the answer. Because it would be weird. But, oddly, I'm dying to see how he acts around other girls. The romantic side of him I've never seen before.

He quirks a brow. "If I smoldered, you wouldn't be able to resist me. You'd want a kiss, and I can't kiss you. I can't kiss *anyone*."

"Whatever! I would not! Ew." I put my hand on his chest and try to push him, but of course he doesn't budge. He's a solid guy, covered in muscles … muscles I'm reminded of with my hand on his pec.

He grabs my hand and holds it to his chest so I can't grab it back. Brooks looks down at our hands, before tilting his head back up slightly, just enough to peer at me through his dark lashes. It's unfair how thick his lashes are … not to mention the brilliant blue eyes.

My heartbeat speeds up at the look he's giving me. It feels as if he could incinerate me with one scorching glance. A scorching glance that has never been aimed in my direction before. His normally bright, mischievous twinkle is now much darker than usual. Like his eyes are burning straight into my soul. No, we're friends … nothing more. It's probably just the reflection of the fireplace.

Speaking of fire, did someone raise the hot tub temperature? Because my heart is racing like I just played a rousing round of tennis, and it has *never* raced while looking at my best friend.

Without breaking eye contact, he licks his bottom lip lightly before pulling it into his mouth, just barely biting it … like he's thinking deeply about something. Maybe he's about to say something. If I did the same thing, it would look really awkward. When Brooks does it, it's very appealing.

My body feels frozen, entranced by this strange new look he's giving me. He brings his hand up to the side of my face. His fingers find a strand of hair that fell from my bun, then he tucks it behind my ear.

He pulls his hand back slowly, his thumb grazing my cheek as his hand retreats. Internally, I know my body is leaning towards him, but I can't seem to stop myself.

That wine was a really bad idea.

To my surprise, Brooks leans in closer as well. He releases his bottom lip and one side of his mouth pulls up into a smirk before he leans in all the way and gives me a friendly peck on the forehead.

"That's how I get all the girls," he says cockily when he pulls back again and slides all the way over to the other side of the hot tub.

I'm slack-jawed. He did that move without me even realizing what was happening. It's at this moment that I realize I would have *let* him kiss me.

What is wrong with me?! I cannot kiss Brooks. He is my closest friend, *and* we work side by side every day.

This cannot happen. No kissing. Ever.

Unlimited hand holding was our agreement ... and now I see why.

After Brooks almost seduced me, per my stupid request, he changed the subject to his latest designs for knee replacements. Knees are good. Perfectly safe and not at all sexy.

Eventually, the exhaustion from traveling all day hits us and we head back inside to take turns in the shower. Brooks goes first while I call the kitchen staff and request some of the leftovers from dinner to be sent up for a bedtime snack. I need some carbohydrates to soak up the effects of the wine. And I know Brooks was dying to eat some more of that filet mignon.

Not even five minutes after hanging up, there's a knock on the door and I answer it, seeing Harold in the hallway with a silver tray. I thank him and take the tray inside. Setting it on the bed, I sit down and quickly devour an entire slice of tiramisu and a few bites of steak.

When Brooks opens the bathroom door, steam billows out of the room behind him from his shower, and he's shirtless with just a pair of boxers on.

I gulp, glad I now have some food in my stomach so my brain isn't fuzzy. This is Brooks. My best friend since college. My coworker. My business partner.

He's not my type. Never has been. Dark hair is my thing. And guys who are too busy writing poems to work out.

So he has abs and one of those V things? Other girls might be into all that, but not me. Nope. Definitely not into chiseled blonde guys who have the strength and energy to roughhouse with their adorable nieces and nephews.

I take one last glance at his boxers before noticing there's a caution sign printed on the black fabric with words on it. I read the words out loud with barely contained laughter. "Caution, handle with care?" Grabbing a pillow, I throw it at his face.

He catches it easily and tosses it back on the bed. "Shut up!" He chuckles, but his cheeks are just the teensiest bit pink, either from his hot shower, or from embarrassment. "I thought I'd have my own room, remember?"

I cover my mouth with a pillow to muffle my laughter. "Those are so much worse than my nightgown."

He sees the food and his eyes widen with excitement. He rushes toward the bed and sits next to me, picking up a bit of steak with his fingers and popping it into his mouth and then licking his fingers clean. I'm all too aware of the half-naked man on my bed. His thick, leg muscles on full display, the rise and fall of his bare chest ... his tongue licking his fingers.

I shake my head, trying to get my bearings again. "Is that seriously what you're sleeping in?"

He grimaces. "Sorry, I didn't pack any sweats or anything. Just jeans and dressy clothes for the wedding. And boxers to sleep in."

I release a heavy sigh. "This is weirder than I thought it would be." Realizing I said the words out loud, I clamp my mouth shut, hiding behind the pillow again.

Brooks gently grabs the pillow away from me. "Hey, I'm sorry I didn't pack actual pajamas. This is weird for me too. Maybe Preston has something I could borrow?"

I think on it for a moment before responding, "Probably. But we wouldn't be very convincing if we asked to borrow flannel pajamas, would we?"

He looks at me with resignation in his gaze. "Yeah, that's a good point." He worries his bottom lip. "You mentioned going to some antique shops ... Does the town nearby have a store where I could buy something to sleep in?"

My eyebrows draw together as I contemplate his question. "It's a quaint little town, but I think they have some gift shops. Since it's winter, they might have pajamas in stock."

"Perfect," he says before sliding under the covers, pulling them up to his chest so he's mostly covered. "We'll go tomorrow, then?"

"I'll check with Mildred to make sure she doesn't need me tomorrow morning, but it should work." Sliding off the bed, I start walking toward the closet before looking back at Brooks. "All right. My turn for a shower." I feel a little awkward announcing the obvious, but it seems so weird to shower with Brooks right here in the next room.

Ducking inside the walk-in closet, I search for a modest pair of pajamas. I rummage through a myriad of luxurious, silk nightgowns that my mother stocked in the closet for me, and just as I'm about to panic, I find one set of flannel pajamas at the very bottom of the drawer. Thank goodness.

I toss them over my arm and make sure Brooks sees them when I walk out into the main bedroom and then the bathroom. He laughs when he sees the long, plaid fabric.

"You're going to burn up in those things. I'm basically a heater."

I give him an annoyed look then head into the bathroom and lock the door behind me. Not that I think Brooks would barge in, but it makes me feel less vulnerable. Like I can pretend he isn't just on the other side of that wooden door.

Showering quickly, I do my regular nighttime routine ... moisturizer, deodorant, teeth brushing. Then I throw my pajamas on before launching into a pep talk in the mirror about how this isn't weird at all. Lots of girls have muscular, male besties.

It's totally not a big deal. I also curse my mother for not sticking to her usually strict rules about couples having separate bedrooms until marriage. Or at least putting king size beds in all the guest rooms.

When I open the door, I see Brooks sprawled out like a starfish on the bed, no longer underneath the covers.

I raise my eyebrows and he groans. "I'm so hot under these flannel sheets. Aren't your parents rich enough to buy some one-million-thread-count Egyptian-cotton instead?"

"You're such a spoiled baby," I tell him, rolling my eyes and motioning for him to scoot over.

He raises up on his elbows. "Says the girl who has a butler."

I slide under the covers and burrow into them, feeling perfectly warm and cozy. "It's freezing outside! Flannel sheets are warm and comfortable!"

"Flannel sheets are for people who shop at Walmart." He pouts. "Do you have some silk nighties I can sleep on?"

That makes me chuckle. "Actually, there's a drawer full of those babies in the closet."

He quirks a brow. "And you chose those?" He gestures to my plaid set.

"Not all of us are human heaters. I'm cold."

He turns to lay on his side, facing me, then grabs a pillow and makes himself comfortable on top of the blankets. His arm muscles bulge as he grips the pillow, and his long, muscular legs stretch all the way to the end of the mattress.

I turn over so I don't have to look at him. "Goodnight, Brooks," I say in a tone that's a warning to stop talking—er, whining.

He sighs. "Goodnight, muffin butt."

Chapter 17

Brooks

Hearing my alarm ring, I groan. I could easily sleep until noon every day. But I have antiquing to do. I groggily reach for my phone and turn the alarm off. The sound of a hair dryer and then the clanking of cosmetic products comes from the bathroom.

"I guess Molly's already up," I whisper to myself.

Propping myself up to a seated position with pillows, I tap on my family group chat and see there are several missed texts from the group chat, and from Madden.

Windell Family group chat:
Sophie: Ahh, that makes sense!
Mom: You'll be home in time for Christmas, right??

David: If I can fly home all the way from Europe, Brooks can fly home from Vermont.

Dad: Still seems fishy to me, but whatever you say.

I sigh ... I suppose three out of four isn't so bad. I tap out of the thread and read my separate messages from Madden.

Madden: Okay. What's *really* happening?

Madden: *gif of Sebastian the crab tapping his claw and glaring*

I knew Madden would be the toughest to convince, seeing as he's the only one who knows about my feelings for Molly.

Brooks: What do you mean? We're on a business trip.

Madden: Tell me or I'll rat you out to David.

Brooks: Rat me out for what? Being a responsible business owner?

Madden: I'll figure out what's really going on. I have my ways. #CongressmanPerks

Brooks: Fine. She wanted someone to pose as her new boyfriend at her sister's wedding so Todd would leave her alone.

Madden: Wow, I totally thought it was just a business trip. That was too easy.

Brooks: Whatever! Anyway, we won't be kissing or even really dating. So, technically I'm not breaking the rules.

Madden: You think people are going to be convinced she's dating you without you two even kissing?

Madden: *gif of Jim from The Office staring into the camera*

Brooks: Not everything is about sexual attraction. How does Odette put up with you?

Madden: She puts up with me because our sexual attraction is on point.

With a roll of my eyes, I toss my phone onto the bed. Molly finally emerges from the bathroom. She's still in those hideous flannel pajamas, but now her hair is down and curled at the ends, and she has just enough makeup on to enhance her already beautiful features.

"Well, good morning, Mr. Sleepy," she says cheerfully before heading to her closet.

"Morning people are annoying."

She giggles and closes her closet door. She's in there for maybe ten minutes before stepping back out in black leggings and a fitted black sweater. There's a white puffer coat draped over her arm, and her feet look ready for a blizzard in tan snow boots. The brown fur peeking out the top of the boots is begging me to pay attention to her very sexy calves. The snow-bunny look is completed with a white snow hat. A color that contrasts nicely with her dark hair.

"Let me see if Mildred responded about today's schedule," she says, walking to her nightstand and grabbing her phone off of it. She taps the screen a few times then smiles. "Okay, she doesn't need me until two for dress fittings. So we're free to spend the morning antiquing!" Molly looks at me with barely contained excitement in her wide blue eyes and I can't help but smile back at her.

I jump up off the bed and rub my hands together. "Then let's go! Plus, I'm starving."

She smirks and shakes her head slightly. "Are you ever not hungry?"

Chuckling at her comment, I take her coat from her and hold it up so she can slide her arms inside of it. She shrugs the coat on then zips it up. She smells heavenly, her usual scent of Chanel No. 5 and that special Molly scent no one else has. I want to wrap my arms around her waist, pull her into me and burrow my nose into her hair. Thankfully, my stomach growls loudly before I can actually put that thought into action.

Molly turns to look at me, her eyes widening when she realizes I literally just rolled out of bed and am still in my briefs. "Hurry up and get dressed! Before you die of starvation!"

"Okay, okay!" I hold my hands up, urging her to calm down.

She rolls her eyes. "I'll wait for you outside. No lolly-gagging!"

"So bossy," I mutter under my breath. But knowing I'm the only one she's comfortable being bossy with brings me joy. Bossy Molly is also kind of hot.

Molly shoots me a stern look before opening the bedroom door and stepping outside.

After eating at a little cafe that had the most amazing maple syrup I've ever tasted, we walk back into the cold December air. The trees and cars in the small town are covered with snow, but the sidewalks and roads have been cleared. It's a picturesque little village with brick buildings and glass front shops, all featuring Christmas-themed displays.

Molly has coffee from the cafe in one hand—which she swears is *almost* as good as the coffee she makes—and loops her other arm through mine as we walk down the sidewalk. She must be worried she'll see someone she knows. Either that or she's freezing.

"I feel like any moment we're going to meet a woman named Holly who's trying to save the town's Christmas tree farm, just for some big-city schmuck to barge in and try to buy the property from under her so he can build condos on it."

Molly bursts out laughing. "What are you talking about?"

"This town looks like a Hallmark movie waiting to happen," I whisper conspiratorially.

Molly uses her shoulder to shove me, but she's laughing under her breath. A blonde woman dressed in a red velvet dress walks past us. She smiles and says good morning; Molly and I smile back at her.

Once she's out of earshot, I lean in toward Molly's ear. Lowering my voice, I say, "Oh my gosh, that was Holly." I spot a man across the street with a briefcase wearing a long wool trench coat. "And don't look now, but there's her enemy: Christopher Christmas-Balls."

She snickers despite herself. "Brooks," she warns.

"He wants to take the land out from under her. But little does he know that she's going to end up under *him*." I waggle my eyebrows suggestively.

"Brooks!" Molly gasps, pulling her arm from mine and slapping my shoulder with her mittened hand. "I'll never be able to look at these people again!" she whisper-yells.

I laugh at her tiny hand slapping at me, and she starts laughing too. We come to a small antique shop and Molly steps in front of the door, blocking me from entering.

"Can I trust you to behave yourself? This is my favorite shop and I don't want to get banned."

I place my hand over my heart. "Scout's honor."

She rolls her eyes but moves so I can open the door. We walk inside and the warm air from the antique store smells like cinnamon. A little old lady perks up from behind the weathered, wooden counter. "Molly Vanderbilt! I've been expecting you to pop in, what with your sister's wedding and all."

"Good morning, Mrs. Nikolas!"

I shoot Molly a knowing look at the woman's last name. But she ignores me and continues.

"I've been excited to see what you've got since last Christmas," Molly says with an excited glimmer in her eyes. I love seeing her in her old-lady-antiquing element like this.

The tiny woman grins. "Head to the back. You'll love the new tea sets."

Molly squeals and walks down the long aisle to the very back of the store. She disappears behind an arrangement of Victorian dressers.

"So," I lean against the counter and give Mrs. Nikolas my signature smile. "Where might I find some spoons?"

Her eyes light up with recognition, shifting toward the back of the store where Molly disappeared. "Ahh, for her collection? You're a good one."

"The way to a woman's heart is through antiques." I wink.

She sighs dreamily. "Music to my ears. Come this way." Mrs. Nikolas waves for me to follow her and opens a door behind the counter that leads to a messy storage room. "I haven't even put these out yet, but they're perfect for Molly."

I follow closely behind her as she walks to a wooden case on top of some dusty boxes and opens it. Inside the box, nestled in a dark blue velvet, are two spoons. Both silver and polished, one has an ivory cameo on the handle and the other has an intricately carved M.W. on the handle. I know they're just some random person's initials from long ago ... but the first thought that pops into my head is *Molly Windell*.

Chapter 18

Molly

I'm knee-deep in delicate tea towels and hand-painted china when Brooks clears his throat to announce his presence. "Do you need a hand there?"

Turning, I see his arms are extended, so I hand him two of the tea cups I'm currently juggling. "Thanks," I say with a smile. "Where have you been?"

"Just chatting with Mrs. Nikolas. She loves me."

Unsurprised by her falling in love with Brooks, *or* by his cockiness, I shake my head at his comment and continue looking at the china display. "It's so hard to choose. But they won't all fit in my suitcase."

He chuckles at my indecisiveness but holds the cups for me without complaint. Which is more than Todd ever did. He refused to even go antiquing with me. He said, and I quote, "Why buy old crap when we have the money to buy whatever we want?"

His spoiled and entitled attitude didn't bother me when we got together in high school, but it was something that became irritating over the years. The more I interacted with people outside of my and Todd's families, the more I realized I didn't want to be that way.

"Do you hate antiquing?" I ask Brooks before I can stop myself.

His head jerks up in surprise. "Of course not. Why would you ask that?"

I sigh. "Sorry. It's just … Todd always thought it was stupid, and I wondered if you felt that way too."

His eyebrows draw together the way they always do when Todd comes up in conversations. "The house I grew up in is literally an antique. I always loved growing up there; it was like everything in the house told a story, and had a special history. That's how I see this, too. You're an old soul. I love that about you. I always have," he says honestly, his eyebrows relaxing.

My heart lightens at his words. "Thank you. I think you've always understood me better than anyone else."

We look at each other for a few seconds, the moment turning serious, maybe even … intimate? No, that can't be the right word. Things between me and Brooks are just usually more lighthearted than this, so it feels strange.

In an attempt to lighten the mood, I add, "That must be why we're such great friends."

Something passes over his expression briefly before he smiles, almost like my words pained him. But it's gone so soon I wonder if I imagined it.

Selecting my favorite three teacups and saucers along with two embroidered tea towels, we walk back up to the front and check out. I give Mrs. Nikolas a hug goodbye and so does Brooks. She squeezes his arm and winks at him before we leave and I can't help but smile ... I can't take him anywhere.

Once we're back outside, I direct us toward a gift shop a few stores down. "Okay, this shop should have some pajamas for you. And possibly sheets." I give him a pointed look filled with judgment at his sensibilities.

He purses his lips before opening the door for me. The gift shop is decorated in red and black buffalo plaid. There's a fire blazing in a wood-burning stove, filling the building with the smell of firewood. It's very homey, but I can only imagine the fit Mildred will throw later when we're at our dress fitting and I smell like a bonfire.

Brooks takes a few long strides toward a wall lined with men's clothing. Mostly t-shirts and hoodies that say *Vermont* on them. He rummages through them before finally finding a rack of clearance pajamas.

He looks through the entire rack before glancing at me with a very annoyed expression. "They're all footie pajamas."

I roll my lips together to keep from laughing. Walking toward him, I spot a pair of white footie pajamas that resembles a unicorn costume. There's even a hood with a unicorn horn attached. I hold it up to him.

"This one would be perfect. Very magical."

He crosses his arms and looks down at the unicorn pajamas. "I'm man enough to wear a unicorn outfit ... but I will literally sweat to death in that furry thing."

I nod once in agreement. "True. Are you sure this is all they have?"

A door at the back of the small shop with a sign reading "employees only" opens up. A burly man with a thick brown beard and snow hat walks out. "Oh, hello! Sorry, I didn't hear you come in!" His deep voice booms heartily throughout the small space. "I'm Otto. How can I help you folks?"

Brooks shoves the unicorn pajamas away from him. "I'm looking for some pajamas ... preferably nothing fuzzy."

Otto puts his large fists on his ample hips and blows out a deep breath, causing his mustache to flutter. "I had some cotton sets last week, but I'm afraid we're all sold out."

Brooks glances at me apologetically before turning his attention back to Otto. "How about sheets?"

"You're in luck!" Otto releases a jolly chuckle and waves us over toward a large wooden shelf displaying several sheet sets tied into cute bundles. "We just restocked our sheets."

They're all flannel. Every single one of them. Brooks politely peruses the selection, anyway.

"I'll be up front. You folks let me know if you need help finding anything else!" Otto says with a grin.

We thank him and he leaves us to look at the sheets. Brooks closes his eyes and groans. "Are there *any* other shops that might have something?"

"You'd have better luck ordering something online. But fair warning, Amazon delivery takes more than two days around here."

"Well, you're just going to have to deal with the boxers then."

The thought of seeing my best friend in nothing but his skivvies every night sends me into a panic. I'm still reeling from the sight of all those muscles last night ... and then again this morning. No, he cannot continue sleeping like that. Our friendship can't survive it.

"If I ask my mother if there are any other sheets, will you wear pajamas?"

"Fine," he concedes. "But I can't wear fuzzy pajamas *and* sleep under flannel or I'll sweat to death."

I cringe. "Gross."

He shoots me a tight smile before walking back to the pajama rack and pulling the unicorn onesie back out.

I bite my bottom lip, trying so hard to keep a straight face ... but a giggle erupts from my mouth. "You're actually going to wear that?"

"It's the only size large they have left!" he says defensively.

Internally, I prepare myself to see my bestie in his briefs again tonight. Because the man's temperature runs hot, and there's no way he can sleep in that fluffy onesie. But the fact he's even willing to put it on to make me feel more comfortable ... gives me that weird little flurry in my belly.

The flurry that needs to go away and never come back. Because flurries for Brooks Windell won't lead to anything good.

Mildred slips out from the dressing room, looking like the queen that she is. Her ballgown-style wedding dress fits perfectly around her tiny waist.

Everyone in the room, including myself, gasps.

My mother rushes toward her. "Mildred Annelise, you're a vision! You're absolutely perfect." She places her hands on Mildred's waist, wearing a look of concentration on her face as if she's internally measuring my sister. "You know," she begins before getting a dreamy, far-off look in her eyes. "When I married your father, my waist was nineteen inches. Can you believe that?" She huffs out a laugh after her humble brag. "He could literally wrap his hands around my waist and his fingers would touch each other!"

Mildred looks at me with a knowing, albeit annoyed, glance. We've heard this a million times. My mother has a master's degree, two daughters, and has helped my father grow his insurance company exponentially. But her crowning achievement in life? (According to her.) Having a nineteen-inch waist twenty-something years ago.

Mildred smiles at our mother before brushing off her comment and continuing to admire herself in the mirror.

My sister's other two bridesmaids and I are squished onto a white couch in the town's only bridal boutique. They were kind enough to let us use the space even though Mildred ordered all the dresses from a designer in France. The shop is tiny but cute, decorated in bright whites with gold accents. They have some gorgeous dresses here too, but, of course, they weren't good enough for my sister.

I've never even met my sister's other bridesmaids, and I'm pretty sure she chose them for their looks more so than their relationship to her. I'm the only brunette in the room, which makes me thankful Mildred hasn't asked me to dye my hair blonde … yet. The aesthetic is important after all. My mind goes to Brooks, wishing I could shoot him a knowing glance and he'd somehow know exactly what I was thinking and we'd both snicker and be reprimanded by my mother.

Trying to get Brooks out of my head, I stand and walk up to my sister. "You really are the most gorgeous bride," I say honestly, because she's bridal-magazine-level perfection.

She grins and smooths her hands down her hand-beaded dress. "Thanks, Molly."

The seamstress comes over and ensures everything is just right and shows us how to bustle the long train on the back of the gown before Mildred sweeps back into the dressing room with a few shop assistants.

When she returns, my mother shoos me and the other bridesmaids into the dressing rooms. "Now, the bridesmaids. Everyone must look flawless for Mildred's big day!"

I smile tightly, wishing I would've drunk some of that champagne the shop assistants offered me earlier. I know the dress will be gorgeous; I'd expect nothing less since my sister and mother have excellent taste. The feeling of dread is simply because my mother always seems to find some flaw in me, like I'll never be as perfect as my sister.

Grabbing the red silky dress, I glide my fingers over the buttery-soft fabric. It's stunning, and the craftsmanship is amazing. I undress and slip the dress over my head, the fabric tumbles down over my body. The dress dips low in the back, stopping just above my derriere. Tiny straps lace up the back in a criss-cross pattern to my neck, where they connect to a high neckline. It takes me a minute to get the dress laced up, but when I look at the final result, I'm impressed. This is the most incredible dress I've ever worn, and it fits my curves just right. It's sexy yet classy at the same time.

I turn to look at my backside in the mirror. The dress accentuates that area in a very nice way. I nod my approval in the mirror. "Not bad, Vanderbilt, not bad," I mutter to myself. That sounds just like something Brooks would say ... Heat rushes to my cheeks as I recall his comment about me having a good butt. I wonder if he'll notice my butt in this dress?

I roll my eyes at the thought, because of course he won't. We don't look at each other like that. Or at least I never did until this past week. This fake boyfriend thing is getting to my head.

I take a deep breath and open the curtain to show the dress to my mother and sister. The other two brides-maids are already dressed. Their names sound exactly the same, but I can't remember what they were ... Kinsleigh and Kayleigh? Marleigh and Beverleigh? Definitely something ending in *eigh*.

Mildred squeals, jumping up and down and clapping her hands. My mother rubs her temples and places an arm on her shoulder, urging her to stop. "Darling, my nerves cannot handle the shrieking."

Mildred ignores her and rushes toward us. "Oh my gosh, you girls look hot! Not as hot as I look in my dress. But still, super hot." She twirls one finger in the air. "Spin for me!"

We all do a little spin to humor her, striking poses and being ridiculous. She squeals again, causing my mother to grimace dramatically. "You guys are going to look so great with your bouquets!"

My mother comes over toward me like a lynx stalking its prey ... or judging it. I swallow slowly, steeling myself for her commentary. She absentmindedly taps her index finger on her lower lip as she studies me. Once she's walked a full circle around me, she finally speaks. "Sweetheart." She lowers her voice, "Yours is a little tight in the back." She shakes her head and gives me a sympathetic look. "We may want to eat a little less tiramisu, hm?"

Mildred and the other girls pretend not to hear her remark, but I can see their subtle glances in our direction.

"Right," I huff out an uncomfortable laugh. "Only protein shakes for me for the next few days, huh?" The words come out sounding a lot more sarcastic than I had planned.

My mother flinches at my words, like she's surprised I'd disagree with her. And usually I wouldn't, at least not outwardly. Brooks must be rubbing off on me.

"Well," she says in a snippy tone. "We better get back to the cabin in time to greet the rest of the wedding party. Everyone should arrive within the hour." She looks directly at me as she says it. I can only assume she's hinting that I should be there to welcome Todd. Except he has his own date, so that would be incredibly weird.

I smile at her in response, not knowing what to say.

Chapter 19

Brooks

The rest of the day, I'm on my own. I use the time to conference call Hope back at the office and make sure everything is running smoothly, and to do some more research on my knee replacement design. With Molly also being out this week, we'd already given our staff the week off. Hope agreed to go in a few times and check the messages.

Around six in the evening, Molly finally arrives back at the room. Her shoulders are slumped, her pretty mouth is set in a frown. She looks completely and utterly exhausted. I want to pull her into my arms. For her to allow me to carry the weight of whatever is bothering her on my shoulders.

I close my laptop and set it on the nightstand before standing from the bed. "You okay?"

She straightens her posture and smiles at me. The smile doesn't reach her eyes … I'm not sure it even reaches her mouth. It's so fake.

I glare at her. "Don't hide from me, Molly. What's wrong?"

Her chin trembles slightly and that's when my resolve melts. I take a few steps toward her, wanting so badly to hold her.

Contemplating for a moment, I give in partially, and place my hands on each side of her arms. She doesn't pull away from me, so I relax and allow my thumbs to rub back and forth, which I hope is a comforting caress.

She takes a slow, steadying breath. "Today was just a lot. Between Todd and his family arriving, and then my mother being, well, my mother …" She closes her eyes and takes a deep breath. "All I want to do is take a hot shower and listen to some music that my mother would hate. But we have to go down to dinner. Everyone will be there."

My hands are still on her arms. I'm internally elated. She's allowing me to touch her and doesn't seem bothered by it, so I don't remove my hands. "We don't *have* to do anything. Let's skip dinner. Tell them we're sick."

She gives me an endearing look. "Oh, Brooks. I wish we could. But if I hide in my room all night, they win."

"What did they say to you?" I ask, wondering what I missed while I was upstairs.

Molly releases a heavy sigh. "Todd's parents pulled me aside and told me their son uprooted his entire life to follow me to Kansas, and that I can't just throw it all away on a pretty face."

I snort. "Am I the pretty face?"

Molly rolls her eyes but laughs. "Obviously. And it's so ridiculous that they think I made him follow me. I was fully prepared to either try long distance ... or to end things. And that was almost three years ago! Why bring it up now?"

"Yeah, that's ridiculous they're blaming you when he literally has his own date with him. Not to mention someone he was with before you guys even broke up. He disgusts me," I grit out that last part.

Every time I think about Todd cheating on Molly, I have to work hard not to let my temper get the best of me. Besides, getting into a fight with Turd Da Punk wouldn't even be challenging enough to make it worthwhile. It would be like Godzilla battling it out with a sea otter.

She takes a small step back, and I release my hands from her arms. "Don't let it get to you, okay? Let me change and we can just get this over with and then relax in the hot tub."

I relax my shoulders, trying to show her I'm calm, but my jaw is still clenched. Molly walks into the closet to change, and I take the opportunity to calm down. After a few deep breaths, I'll hopefully be back to my charming self for dinner.

Molly steps out of the closet in tights, heeled black boots, and a grey tweed shift dress. She looks like the prettier and more modern version of Audrey Hepburn. I'm beginning to wonder if that closet is some kind of magical, sexy, outfit generator.

"You look great." I smile and her demeanor seems a little more positive now. She smiles back at me, her eyes dropping to my tie.

"Another bow tie, huh?"

"I can change," I say quickly, moving toward the dresser.

She moves in front of me. "No, don't. If they don't like your adorable bow ties, that's their problem."

Adorable. You wouldn't think the word *adorable* would make a man's heart race... but that's what it's doing to me. I grin in spite of my desire to play it cool. Molly chuckles and loops an arm through mine, dragging me toward the door.

We arrive in front of the doorway that leads into the dining room, and I remove Molly's hand from my arm so I can hold her hand. I interlace our fingers the way I've always wanted to, and our hands fit so perfectly together it's like magic. She glances up at me briefly, a look of surprise on her face. I'm not sure if it's because I'm holding her hand, or if she's also noticed how well we fit.

Everyone else is already seated at the table. Preston and Mildred are on one side with Preston's family. On the opposite side sits Todd and Trudy, along with another couple who I can only assume are Todd's parents. Todd and Preston's fathers look alike, so much so that they could pass as twins.

Molly's father is at the head of the table with Mrs. Vanderbilt seated next to him. Two blonde girls are next to her. I'm assuming they're the other two bridesmaids?

Molly and I make our way to the only two seats left, which are right next to one of the blonde girls. She takes a moment to introduce me to the other bridesmaid. Their names are generic ones that sound the same and I instantly forget what they are. They blush and look me up and down, giggling and whispering to each other as if I'm not standing right here with my supposed girlfriend.

By society's standards, they're pretty enough. But just like all the women I've dated in the past, not nearly as beautiful as Molly. In comparison, they're lackluster and disappointing.

Nothing wrong with them really, other than the fact they're not Molly Vanderbilt.

I pull Molly's chair out for her and look across the table to see Todd and his entire family glaring at me in unison. I've never met his family, but they're all dark and dramatic looking ... They remind me of the living version of the Addams family. How does Molly even fit in with these people?

Molly's family is uptight, sure. But do they have anything in common with Todd's family besides money? If so, what a horrible reason to be friends.

I'm not totally naive. I realize people often find camaraderie with those similar to themselves—my family not excluded. I mean, we know everyone at our local country club. But we don't actively entertain people we don't genuinely like. We're polite, of course. But we're not going to invite someone to our tee time just because of their net worth.

Kinsleigh and Kayleigh, or whatever the heck their names were, are still giving me flirtatious glances. When I take my seat next to Molly, I make sure to drag her chair as close to mine as possible, and then I drape my arm over the back of hers.

Ignoring the blondes next to her, I lean in close and whisper, "You're the most beautiful girl in the room."

Making sure to be loud enough the two girls next to us can hear.

She pulls back to look at me and rolls her eyes, but I can't help but notice the pretty blush on her cheeks. I wink at her. I'm sure she thinks this is all for show, but she really is the most beautiful girl in the room.

I'm not pretending.

Leaning back in, I place a kiss on top of her head, lingering there for a moment to inhale the scent of her shampoo.

Mr. Vanderbilt stands from his seat, clearing his throat so he gets everyone's attention. "So glad to have everyone here for Mildred and Preston's nuptials. Thank you all for coming, and please let us know if we can do anything to make your stay more comfortable."

Todd scoffs, looking directly at me. He looks like he wants to say his stay would be more comfortable if I wasn't here. His date, Trudy, looks up at him in confusion. She tugs on his arm and he turns his attention to her, forcing a smile. She grins back and snuggles in closer to him.

Molly's dad sits back down and the side doors open, allowing half a dozen servers in, each carrying the same silver trays they did last night. Once we all have our meals in front of us, the staff silently usher back out. I wonder to myself how they do that so silently... Like, is there an old, British woman downstairs training them all? I'm picturing a scene from that show Sophie loves … What's it called? *Downton Abbey?*

I'm pulled from my thoughts when I glance down and see Molly's meal is different from mine. I lean over slightly to get a look at the other bridesmaid's meals. Sure enough, Molly has a salad and ice water while everyone else at the table was served fettuccine alfredo and wine.

A server comes into the room with several bottles of wine and a white towel draped over his forearm. I crook my finger at him.

His eyes shift to the Vanderbilts at the head of the table. When he sees they're distracted in conversation, he walks over. "Can I help you, sir?"

"Yes, Molly didn't get her full meal. Could you bring another out?"

Molly's head snaps up to meet mine. She widens her eyes as if silently conveying a message. "What?" I ask, and she sighs heavily.

Her mother speaks from the head of the table. "Matthew, dear. Molly only wants a salad this evening. She must not have communicated that to her … friend."

The young server, Matthew, darts his eyes from Mrs. Vanderbilt then back to me. Finally, he sets his eyes on Molly. "Miss Vanderbilt, is the salad to your liking, or can I get you some pasta as well?"

She smiles at him but her eyes look conflicted. I don't know what the full story is here, but it's obvious she wants to tell him she wants pasta, but she's holding back. Which leads me to believe her mother, for some reason, requested Molly not be given pasta. My head swivels slowly to look at Mrs. Vanderbilt. Who's narrowing her eyes at me.

If Molly wants carbohydrates, Molly gets carbohydrates. I narrow my eyes back at her.

"I'd love some pasta, thank you, Matthew," Molly finally responds, her voice sounding nervous.

"My pleasure." He bows his head and rushes from the room before Mrs. Vanderbilt orders his beheading.

Chapter 20

Molly

Matthew comes back with a plate of pasta and sets it in front of me. The plate shakes. He's obviously terrified of defying a direct order from my mother. I cannot believe she told them not to give me anything but salad tonight. I should've known she'd do that. She won't be happy until I'm a size two blonde.

"What the hell is going on? Do I need to have a talk with your mother?" Brooks whispers in my ear.

His close proximity is making my tummy do that swirling thing again. Wow, he smells good. I'm probably just hungry, I tell myself. Anything would smell good right now. Well, anything except salad with no dressing.

"I appreciate you wanting to come to my rescue, but please just leave it be. I have my pasta now, so you're already my hero," I tell him quietly, then pat his cheek affectionately for show.

He gently grabs my wrist and leans into my caress. When I think he's going to release my hand, he instead pulls it back just enough to place a kiss on my palm, allowing his lips to rest there for a second. His eyes don't leave mine during this entire interaction, and I can't help but blush at the intimacy of it. When he releases my hand, I can still feel the warmth of his kiss on my palm, as if I've been branded by him.

This man is making me swoon, one carbohydrate at a time. And it has to stop.

Once we've all finished our dinner, dessert is brought out ... for everyone except me. I glance nervously at Brooks, who has probably put everything together by now. Sure enough, his eyes are closed like he's trying to stay calm, and his jaw is clenched tightly. He opens his eyes with an exhaled breath, cocking his head to the side and popping his very thick, muscled neck. He looks as if he's about to enter an arena and kick somebody's butt. Seeing as the other person in that arena would be my mother, I pat his thigh under the table.

"Stay calm. I don't want to make a scene," I tell him quietly. He adjusts his ridiculous bow tie, this one with little Highland cow heads all over it, and his cheerful demeanor returns. I feel myself relax.

Brooks scoots his dessert nearer to me, picks up his fork, and scoops up a bite of chocolate cake. He glances at my mother quickly before looking back at me and guiding the fork to my mouth.

I open my mouth to tell him I'm not hungry, but he slides the bite of cake into it. He smiles, obviously trying not to laugh. I play along and try to make this cake feeding thing look as romantic as possible.

Closing my eyes, I hum my approval as the delicious cake melts in my mouth. "That's decadent," I say in my sultriest voice.

Brooks continues smirking and reaches a hand up to my face. He swipes at my bottom lip with his thumb. When he pulls it back, I see a dollop of chocolate frosting that must've been on my mouth. Right when I think I've ruined the whole charade with my messy face, he brings his thumb to his mouth and slowly licks the frosting off.

I hear the other bridesmaids next to me sigh. Probably wishing they had all this masculine attention on themselves. He winks at me, then scoops up another bite of cake. I eat this bite more gracefully.

Brooks continues feeding me, taking a few bites for himself. And we try not to laugh. All in all, I'd say we were pretty successful.

When I finally look up, I find every single person at the table watching us. Todd's jaw is gaping and his parents look horrified, as do my parents. Preston is smiling in our direction, clearly amused until Mildred notices his smile and elbows him in the side.

"Wow," Brooks announces. "That was the best chocolate cake I've ever tasted." He licks his lips and pats his stomach. "Are you full, Molly? Or do you want some more?"

"I'm good, thank you." I look over at my mother, whose lips are set in a thin, straight line. Her terse look isn't directed on me, though. It's settled firmly on Brooks. Although he seems completely oblivious to her annoyance.

Or at least he's acting like he is.

Brooks drags me up to our room quickly after dinner, most likely wanting to avoid my mother's ire. Once we're up the stairs, he bends at the waist and rests his hands on his knees, breathing in and out dramatically like he just ran a mile.

"Barely made it," he pants, "without murdering your mom." He exhales again. "Managed to keep my temper in check. What's my prize?"

Planting my fists on my hips, I glare at him. "No one is murdering anybody."

"What the hell is her problem? Why wouldn't she let you eat?" He stands up straight, losing his humor and looking at me expectantly.

The man wants answers, and he wants them now.

I sigh and start walking toward our door down the hallway. "She thought my bridesmaid's dress was a little snug." I glance at him over my shoulder briefly, but keep walking.

He quirks an eyebrow. "And what did *you* think?"

I withhold a smile at his question. Brooks always wants to know my opinion on things. Actually, he encourages me to *give* an opinion. Something no one else seems to do.

Biting my bottom lip, I think about how I should answer. But decide to go with honesty because this is Brooks. I don't have to hide my opinions from him. "Actually, I thought I looked kind of, well, sexy."

We make it to our door and he opens it for me with a big grin. "I have a feeling you're right and your mother is wrong."

I laugh, hoping he's correct. "Hot tub time?"

"Hot tub time," he confirms.

Ten minutes later, we have our suits on and are about to go out to the back deck when a knock comes from our door. Brooks looks at me with a worried expression, and I shrug before walking over and opening the door.

Preston and Mildred are there with their swimsuits on. Mildred, of course, in a tiny string bikini, and Preston in pink trunks that have little whales all over them.

"Can we join you?" Mildred asks.

I glance back at Brooks who looks mildly annoyed. "Uh, sure," I say, not wanting to be rude.

Brooks holds the door open to the back deck and we all rush to the hot tub since it's freezing outside and beginning to snow.

Brooks is the last to get in and Preston whistles low and slow, his eyes wide. "No wonder my cousin hates you, man. I think *I* even have a crush on you."

"Right?" Mildred agrees. "His muscles have muscles!"

"Uh, thanks," Brooks says, looking at me with a look that says, *what the hell?*

"So," I begin, trying to change the subject. "What are you guys doing here? I know you have a hot tub on your balcony too."

They glance at each other, both grimacing. "Todd wanted us to hang out with him and Trudy," Preston explains.

"We told them we were going to sleep," Mildred adds. "And their room is right next to ours, so they would've heard us outside. Ugh! Trudy is a hairdresser for goodness' sake." She rolls her eyes like even the idea of conversing with someone so (supposedly) beneath her is appalling.

"What's wrong with hairdressers?" Brooks asks, slinging one muscled arm behind me and toying with a loose tendril of hair that fell from my bun.

Mildred brings a hand to her chest like she's mortified. "Oh goodness, I'm so sorry. You're not a hairdresser are you?"

Brooks eyebrows draw together. "Uh, no. I own a company with Molly. Remember?"

"Oh, right!" She laughs. "I totally forgot."

"But I don't see anything wrong with being a hairstylist. I mean, if it weren't for them, my hair would reach my butt."

Mildred flips her blonde hair over her shoulder as if just remembering her fabulous hair … which is all thanks to her hair stylist. "Oh, true. Good point."

"I still don't want to hang out with them. I don't care what they do for a living," Preston says, wrinkling his nose.

"Isn't he your best man?" Brooks asks, then looks at me with a very confused look.

"Only because my dad made me ask him," Preston admits, sounding like a school boy.

Mildred slaps his chest. "Preston!"

He grimaces. "Oh sorry, I forgot I wasn't supposed to tell anyone that. Our fathers are dual owners in their company … so we have to save face and all."

Mildred's eyebrows go up and focuses on me and Brooks ... specifically his hand that is still playing with the hair at the nape of my neck. "Speaking of co-owning a company ... how does that work with all this?" She motions between me and Brooks with a wave of her hand.

I open my mouth to respond, but Brooks beats me to it. "Molly and I have been friends for six years. Our relationship was first built on friendship, then trust and mutual respect. Adding in romance won't change any of that."

My head swivels to look at him. How did he come up with that on the spot? It's like he had that monologue prepared in advance. He smiles and kisses me on the forehead.

Mildred narrows her eyes. "Hm, alright. But it *could* get tricky."

"How so?" Preston asks.

"Think of all the arguments your father and uncle have gotten into over the years. What if they weren't brothers, but a husband and wife? They would've gotten a divorce ages ago."

"Ah," Preston hums. "You're right. A romance between two people who own the same company is a recipe for disaster."

My heart tightens at their comments. I'm not sure why; Brooks and I aren't even in a real relationship. So why do their words hurt so much?

"Molly and I aren't your father and uncle," Brooks says confidently, seeming unperturbed by the conversation. He's the picture of cool confidence. "Did you two plan this? Are you trying to convince Molly she'd be better off with Todd?" He chuckles.

I lean forward and look directly at my sister. "Oh my gosh, is that what this is? Did Mom send you?"

"No!" Mildred insists. "Although we all know you and Todd will get back together eventually."

Preston's face falls. "Why? I like Brooks better."

Mildred turns and shushes him. "You're not helping."

Brooks relaxes and leans back again, the side of his body brushing against mine under the hot water. His hand that's been toying with my hair drops to my shoulder. "Why would you want your sister to be with someone who treats her like garbage? I'm honestly wondering."

Mildred huffs an annoyed sigh. "Listen, you probably do well for yourself and everything ... But as Vanderbilts, we're accustomed to a certain ... level of comfort."

"So she'd be better off with billions of dollars than someone who treats her with love and respect?"

Prestons chuckles. "Todd will grow up a lot once he finally gets his trust fund."

Mildred gasps. "Preston!"

He grimaces. "Oh shit, I wasn't supposed to say that."

My eyebrows shoot up at his comment. "Wait, Todd hasn't received his trust fund? Why?"

"You've done it now," Mildred whisper-yells.

"I'm sorry, baby!" He grovels.

Brooks and I look at each other; he looks just as confused as I am. We wait a moment for them to finish arguing before I ask my question again, "*Why* hasn't he received his trust?"

Mildred glares at Preston and he begrudgingly explains, "Well, Todd was rather ... reckless ... with money and girls throughout high school. My uncle and aunt were terrified to send him to college because of it. They worried he'd be in the press all the time, causing drama. My father sat down with Todd's and they came up with the idea to put a marriage clause in his trust. They thought it would help him make better decisions."

The blood drains from my face as I start putting the pieces together. "That's right when he started dating me."

Preston glances at Mildred, then back to me. "You were always so responsible, and sweet. Our families sort of encouraged him to date you. Thinking you'd be a good influence."

I swallow, my throat feeling thick and dry. Tears sting my eyes, but I don't let them fall. "Why didn't he just marry me and get his trust fund then?"

Mildred ends her silence. "He has until he's twenty-seven to get married. But his dad pays him way too much for the work he does remotely." She rolls her eyes. "So apparently he hasn't been very motivated to get his trust before then."

"Did his parents make him follow me to Kansas, too?" I ask. Mildred and Preston's faces grow serious and they avoid my gaze. "Well, that answers that question," I say bitterly.

My feeling of shock and hurt slowly turns in my gut until I just feel angry ... really angry. "You kept this from me and let me waste seven years of my life thinking he cared about me?"

She has the good sense to look ashamed. "As your big sister, I just wanted you to be taken care of."

I stand and start to get out of the hot tub, and Mildred stands too, grabbing my arm. "Please! Try to understand. I thought he'd grow up by now and want to settle down."

Pulling my arm away, I step out of the hot tub and grab a towel. "Settle down, or settle?"

Brooks gets out of the hot tub, taking my towel and wrapping it around me. I'm thankful for his assistance since my hands are trembling.

Mildred and Preston quickly step out of the hot tub and grab towels. "Molly, please. I'm sorry. Explaining this all out loud definitely makes it sound ..."

"Crazy? Insane? Inexplicable?" Brooks offers, his voice deep and demanding. He's standing between me and my sister, like a bodyguard. Solid as a brick wall, un-moving in his desire to protect me.

Mildred's chin quivers. I'm not sure if it's because she's cold or if she's trying to hold back tears. "Well, yes. All of those things."

I scoff. "You didn't think I deserved to have what you and Preston have? Is the measure of a man really his net worth?" I throw my hands up in frustration. "Ugh, I can't even continue this conversation."

Mildred and Preston both start speaking at once, but Brooks holds a hand up to stop them. "I think it's best we end the evening here." His tone is firm, and no one bothers arguing with him.

Preston urges Mildred toward the patio door. She's reluctant, studying my face and looking like she's about to speak again. Preston gives her one more nudge, and she silently turns and leaves.

Chapter 21

Brooks

Senior Year MIT

"Okay, I know this is crazy ... but hear me out."

Molly eyes me wearily from where she's sitting on her bed. We just finished our senior project, and between our laptops, books, and papers, the floor is barely visible.

"Continue," she says.

"The breast implants we designed are good. Really good. We could use this design in real-life," I explain, standing up from my seat on the ground and moving to sit on the edge of her bed. "One of my dad's med school buddies is a plastic surgeon. I sent him our design, and he thought it was incredible. He said the shape and material would work so well and the texture we added would look really natural."

She smiles. "Of course it is! You're a brilliant engineer, Brooks. The top biomedical engineering companies are going to be fighting over you."

"That's where the crazy part comes in." I drag a hand through my blonde hair, which needs to be trimmed badly. "I don't want to work for someone else's company."

Her smile falters, and she closes her laptop, giving me her full attention. "Wait, what?"

"We should start our own company. You and me."

Her mouth opens like she's about to say something but it just stays open and no words come out. She makes a weird strangled sound and blinks several times. "That's a huge commitment ... we'd need permits, and licenses, and FDA approvals."

I nod my head as she makes her list. This is why we'd be great running a company together. We can both design medical equipment, sure. But Molly *also* has a brain for business.

Her eyes flit around the room like her brain is going crazy with the possibilities. "And where? You're from Kansas, and I'm from Massachusetts."

"I'll move wherever." I shrug. "But I believe in this design, and I think we'd be brilliant together." Realizing how that sounded, I add, "running a company."

Although we'd be brilliant together in every aspect. But I'll keep that to myself.

She inhales a deep breath and blows it out slowly, causing her bangs to fly up. "Give me some time to think about it and research. It is a crazy idea ... but I'm not saying no." Her mouth pulls up in an apprehensive smile.

"That's all I'm asking." I lean toward her slightly and hold her gaze. "But Molly? When you're thinking about it, don't think about what other people *want* you to do. Consider what *you* want."

She looks at me thoughtfully, her mind trying to grasp exactly what I'm saying. I need to really spell this out for her. "I know you hate causing drama, or ruffling anyone's feathers ... and that's admirable. But this is your future, *your* life. It doesn't matter what I or Todd or your parents want you to do. Your opinion is the only one that counts."

Her eyes sparkle like she's about to cry. She clears her throat and squirms as if my words made her uncomfortable. "Yeah, okay. I will."

Molly

It's been two days since my conversation with Brooks, and I've hardly slept. All I can think about is starting a business with him. I cannot get it out of my head.

That's not the reason I can't sleep though ... It's because I want to go for it. And because I believe in what we could build. And Brooks knows me well enough to know what would hold me back.

My family, and Todd. I know my parents want me to stay in the area, never use my degree, and settle down with Todd. We will have a boy and a girl and live out the rest of our lives in luxury and comfort.

But what do *I* want? Marriage and kids sound great, but I'm twenty-one. Isn't there time to do this thing with Brooks first? What if I had my own legacy to pass down to my children, and not just my father's?

And Brooks and I work so well together. Not only would it be incredibly fun working with my best friend every day, but with my business sense and his biomedical engineering genius, we'd be amazing. The next GE Healthcare.

I take a sip of my latte just as Todd walks inside the MIT campus coffee shop where I've been waiting for him. He smiles and walks over to my table. He's handsome today with his neatly combed dark hair and dress shirt with sweater vest.

He leans in to kiss my cheek, and I get a whiff of a sweet scent, something that smells feminine and very unlike Todd's cologne. I inhale as he pulls away.

"What's that scent?"

He lowers his head to sniff his own shoulder and then shrugs, avoiding eye contact. "I was shopping for perfume for my mom before this... so I probably still smell like perfume."

He's being weird. Maybe he was buying me a gift and wants to keep it a secret? I put it out of my mind. "So, I have some news," I say excitedly, even though I know he's probably not going to be excited.

"Yeah?" His eyebrows rise.

Rolling my lips together, I steady myself. I want to tell him my plan with confidence so he can't talk me out of it. "I'm going into business with Brooks after graduation."

"Brooks?" He scoffs. "Will we ever be rid of that guy?"

"Todd, he's my best friend. You should try to get to know him!"

He wrinkles his nose at the idea and I continue, "I've been researching, and I think it's best for us to start our company in Kansas."

"Kansas?" He leans his elbows on the table and buries his face in his hands. "You've gotta be kidding me."

"Kansas has cheaper property taxes and business insurance. It just makes sense to start the company there."

He brings his head back up to look at me. "What do you care about saving money, Molly? You have plenty of money. And I'm not moving to Kansas and socializing in barns with overalls-clad country bumpkins."

I roll my eyes. I knew he'd be like this. "Well, you don't have to follow me to Kansas. We've been together for years; we could totally manage a long distance thing for a bit."

He scoffs. "A bit?"

I grimace. "Well, a few years most likely."

"So basically you're breaking up with me to go corn-picking with Brooks Windell?" He crosses his arms and scowls.

"That's Iowa."

He sniffs haughtily. "What?"

"Iowa is known for corn. Kansas is known for wheat." I shake my head, frustrated that we're getting off track. "Anyway, we don't need to break up. You're being dramatic. We can make this work!"

The look on his face tells me he's not convinced. "What if I don't want to do long distance?"

My heart clenches inside my chest that he'd give up on us so easily, but I continue with confidence. "Well, you're welcome to come to Kansas with me."

He leans forward and looks at me with a challenge in his gaze. "And what if I don't want to come to Kansas?"

I flinch, his words feeling like a slap in the face. I would never force him to move to Kansas with me, but does he care so little that he won't even consider it? My hands are shaking, but I try to remain confident, even though I don't feel it. I can't back down, not this time. "I guess you need to do some thinking and decide what you want."

"Yeah, I guess I do." He gets up and leaves the coffee shop without another word.

I continue sipping my latte and try not to cry.

Chapter 22

Brooks

When Molly gets out of the shower, I'm in bed in my unicorn onesie, waiting for her. She appears from the bathroom in a baggy t-shirt, furry pink socks, and her hair wrapped up in a white towel. She cracks a smile when she sees me, which is what I was hoping for after that admission from her sister.

Molly huffs out a breath through her nose, and at first I think she's laughing ... but a second later, her chin quivers and her eyes fill with tears.

I jump out of bed and consider—for the millionth time—pulling her into my arms. She wipes at her tears, trying in vain to dry her face, but more tears keep coming. I reach out to her, but she waves me off, trying to smile. "I'm sorry. I'll be fine, I promise."

She steps around me and crawls into bed, pulling the covers all the way up to her face. Walking around to my side of the bed, I get in as well. I feel unsettled, like I can't calm down unless I hold her. But this isn't about me.

She turns the lamp off on her nightstand so we are immersed in darkness. But I can still hear her quiet sobs. My heart literally aches, wanting so badly to comfort her, but not knowing how.

Eventually, her sobs slow down. Right when I think she's asleep, I feel her hand slide into mine. It's clammy and cold, and I instantly cover it with both of my large, warm hands. I'm half-blissful oblivion and half-heartbroken ... because the girl of my dreams is right here next to me, holding my hand. But she's hurting, and I hate that.

Her voice echoes through the darkness, just loud enough for me to hear. "I can't believe I wasted all those years. On someone who only wanted me as a backup plan for his trust fund."

"I'm so sorry," I tell her, not knowing what else to say.

She hesitates, then I hear her shaky voice again. "You tried to tell me, and I refused to listen."

I rub her hand between mine, trying to warm it up. "Don't do this to yourself. It's in the past. The future is what matters."

She groans. "Yeah, but Brooks. That's *seven* years of my life, wasted. On that ... that ... asshole!"

I gasp. "Mary Elizabeth Vanderbilt. Did you just curse?"

Molly huffs out a laugh. It's small, barely even audible. "Yeah. Not gonna lie, it felt weird."

I make a clicking sound with my tongue, admonishing her, hoping to make her laugh again. Or at least smile. "What is that, about 1.2 million in your mother's swear jar?"

She quirks a brow. "It's a swear *vase*."

"Rare crystal?"

"Of course," she deadpans.

I smile into the darkness, wishing I could see her face. Her voice sounds a little smoother now, like she's no longer crying. "Thanks for making me laugh. I needed that."

The bed moves, and I realize her shoulders are shaking. I think she's crying again, but her shoulders begin to shake even harder ... with hysterical laughter instead of sobs.

"What is so funny?" I ask her.

She's laughing so hard she can barely breathe. "It's just—" More laughter. "You look—" She laughs again. "Absolutely ridiculous."

I start laughing too because she's right. I do look ridiculous. Plus, I'm thrilled she's laughing instead of crying. I don't even care if it's at my expense. My only complaint is, between the onesie and the flannel sheets, I'm sweating profusely here.

Molly flicks her lamp on just in time to watch a bead of sweat drip down my face. "I'm so sorry I forgot to ask my mother about the sheets. You might as well take that thing off or you're going to die of a heat stroke."

"Bless you," I tell her, jumping out of the bed and stripping the unicorn onesie off my sweaty body.

"Oh my gosh, are those ... logs?" I follow her gaze to my boxer briefs. Tonight's are navy-blue and have logs printed all over them, along with the words, "timber loading zone."

I grin. "Oh, yeah. They were a gift from Madden last Christmas."

"What did Diane have to say about that?" she asks.

Chuckling, I get back on the bed, but not under the covers, and lean back against the headboard. "She was horrified, of course. It was awesome."

She shakes her head in dismay. "Brooks and Molly, disappointing mothers everywhere since the day they were born."

"Hey now, these were all Madden's idea!"

Molly laughs, but there's still sadness in her eyes. "Yeah, true. And your mom totally adores you."

"She adores *you* too. You're easy to adore, Molly." I pause, thinking carefully about my next words. "I'm sorry you've been around people who didn't show you that."

She gives me a smile that's so small and so sad, that right in this moment, I promise myself I will spend the rest of my days convincing her she's the most beautiful, intelligent, witty, wonderful, sexy woman on the planet.

I am now Molly's personal entourage, her protector, her goodtime boy.

My sole purpose in life is now making it known to the universe that Molly Vanderbilt is the cat's meow.

ele

The following morning, we head down to breakfast ... a very silent, very awkward breakfast. Preston and Mildred keep glancing at Molly, waiting for her to acknowledge them, but she does an impressive job at ignoring them.

Finally, she turns her attention to her mother. "Oh, I keep forgetting to ask you. Do we have some sheets that aren't flannel?"

Mrs. Vanderbilt's eyebrows raise. "But the flannel ones are your favorite. I was sure to tell the maids to give you those exact ones."

"I do love them. Thank you for being so thoughtful," she says dryly, making me wonder if she's completely over this trip already. "It's just that Brooks's body temperature runs warmer than the rest of the world's, and he's burning up in those sheets."

I smile bashfully. "She's right. I'm sorry for the inconvenience."

Mr. And Mrs. Vanderbilt both stare at me like I'm a disgusting, sweaty pig. Maybe if they ate real food instead of just protein shakes, they wouldn't be so cold all the time.

"I'll have the maids double-check, but I believe we've used all the satin sheets for the other guest rooms. We have extra sheets, of course, but since we're always at the cabin in the winter ... they're all flannel."

Mr. Vanderbilt jumps in, trying to help out. "You might check the shops in town."

Molly gives me an apologetic smile and I give one right back ... because she's about to see my entire quirky underwear collection. Why can't I buy normal underwear? Just plain, black Calvin Kleins or something?

Molly must notice my embarrassed expression. She leans in close and whispers, "All of your underwear are weird, aren't they?"

"Yep," I say quickly, avoiding eye contact.

Todd and Trudy walk in and join Todd's family on the opposite side of the table.

"Ready for your bachelor party tonight?" Todd asks Preston, holding his hand out for a fist bump.

Preston reluctantly bumps it with his own fist and forces a smile. "Can't wait."

Preston's dad leans over and gives them both a pointed look. "You're keeping the bachelor party classy, right, young man?"

"Of course," Todd insists. Todd's father shares a skeptical look with Preston's.

"Brooks," Preston says. "You should join us! Molly will be busy tonight with the bachelorette party, anyway."

Todd makes a strangled sound and glares at Preston.

"Uh, I shouldn't," I say. "I have a lot of work to catch up on."

"Yeah," Todd waves a hand. "He has work to catch up on."

Trudy squeals and claps her hands together. "Oh! Does this mean I can go to the bachelorette party?"

Everyone stops and stares at her. Mildred's eyebrows are nearly to her hairline and her eyes are opened so wide it looks like they might fall out of her head. After last night, torturing Mildred a little doesn't sound so bad, so I decide to go with it.

"You know what? That's a brilliant idea, Trudy. I think I'll join the bachelor party, after all."

I drape an arm casually around Molly's shoulders, and she looks up at me with a knowing grin.

Chapter 23

Molly

After spending the rest of the day at the spa with my mother and the bridal party, I stop by the room to check on Brooks and change for the bachelorette party. I know he had plenty of stuff to catch up on, especially since he was planning on working tonight and now he's going to Preston's bachelor party.

I walk in and he's on the bed, propped up against the headboard with his laptop on his lap. He's wearing a baseball cap, backwards of course, and his earbuds are in his ears.

He smiles when he sees me, closes his laptop, and removes the earbuds. "Hey, how was the spa?"

I sit down on the bed with a sigh. "A little weird after last night. I'm just trying to move past it and not let my feelings ruin Mildred's wedding. It's not her fault after all—it's Todd's." I lay back on the bed and stare up at the ceiling. "And honestly, partially my fault too. I saw all the signs and ignored them."

"You always see the good in people, there's nothing wrong with that," he says. I feel the bed move and look over to see Brooks laying down next to me. He finds my hand and interlaces it with his. His hand is large and calloused, but so warm. I'm surprised by how comforting it is to hold his hand. I'm finding that all of Brooks's little touches are comforting.

He doesn't speak, but just stares at the ceiling with me. He always seems to know exactly what I need, whether it's silence, a dumb joke to make me laugh, or standing up for me when no one else will.

After a few minutes, he looks over at me. "I should probably get changed for the party." He stretches his long limbs before sliding off the bed, removing his cap, then tossing it onto the dresser.

I raise myself up on my elbows. "Why'd you do that?"

He runs his large hand through his hair, messing it up after having it compressed by his hat. "What do you mean?"

Standing, I walk over to the dresser and take his hat before standing in front of him, getting up on my tippy-toes, and placing his hat back on his handsome head. Backwards and all.

He quirks a brow in question. "Uh, pretty sure this isn't in the dress code Preston texted me."

"Doesn't matter." I pull my bottom lip into my mouth, contemplating admitting what I've been thinking about all day. I had way too much free time with my own thoughts between the facial, the waxing, the massage, the nails. Mildred knows how to spoil her bridesmaids, that's for sure. "You don't need to be more like them, or try to fit in to avoid offending anyone. You're the best person I know, Brooks. It's them who should try to be more like *you*."

He blinks slowly, like he's absorbing my words. "I think that's the nicest thing anyone has ever said to me," he admits, his voice sounding more serious than usual.

He wraps his arms around me, pulling me into a big bear hug. My feet lift off the ground and everything. He spins me around and I laugh. "Okay, okay, put me down!"

He listens, allowing me to slide down the front of his firm, well-honed physique. My head spins for a moment at the feel of him against me. I wonder briefly how I ever thought skinny, serious poets were somehow better than sturdy blondes who are built like vikings. Maybe that's how they pillaged so many villages ... The women saw them and simply surrendered.

My viking daydream ends when I notice Brooks is studying me with amused curiosity. I take a step back and bring my hand instinctively to the collar of my sweater. "Well, I'm going to get dressed," I announce a little too loudly.

Brooks smirks like he somehow knows I was picturing him as a viking and that I was happily going to allow him to pillage my township. I walk to the closet, nearly tripping over my own feet. "Get it together, Molly," I whisper to myself. When I finally make it inside the large closet, I close the door and rest my back against it. "What has gotten into you?" I ask myself.

A knock comes from the other side of the door and I jump with a loud gasp. Brooks's voice echoes through the door. "Did you say something?"

"I was talking to myself," I say with a forced laugh. "Ha. You know, just asking myself for fashion advice."

His deep chuckle rumbles through the door and seems to vibrate through my entire body. The viking image comes back to mind before I force myself to think of literally anything else ... rainbows, antique spoons, breast implants, corgis, corgis bow ties ... Brooks's thick neck.

With a groan, I dig my fingers into my hair and pull.

"Are you sure you're okay in there?" Brooks's voice comes through the door again.

"Fine!" My voice sounds strained.

I quickly grab the hot pink dress I saw the other day and put it on. When I saw the pink, I knew it would be perfect for the bachelorette party. The long-sleeved body-con dress is ruched along the sides, creating a flattering silhouette. And since it falls to my mid-calf, I'll stay warm. The top is slightly off-shoulder with a large collar that stretches across my shoulders. With one last glance in the full-length mirror, I decide I'm ready for a girls' night out ... with Trudy.

Somehow knowing how annoyed my sister is about it makes me smile about spending the evening with her. It's not Trudy's fault she's Todd's date. She most likely thinks he's a real catch. I mean, I did... So how can I hold that against her?

When I step out of the closet in my dress and heeled booties, Brooks is standing right outside the closet door with his arms crossed. His blue eyes go wide when he sees me, and it definitely gives me a little thrill of satisfaction.

"Whoah." He twirls his finger, urging me to spin. I oblige, spinning and striking a goofy pose. "Damn. I hope this doesn't cross our friendship boundary, but you look really freaking sexy."

I feel my cheeks heat. "I think we're past worrying about friendship boundaries, don't you? I've seen your punny underwear and everything."

He looks abashed and runs his hand along his chiseled jaw. "Yeah, that's very true."

"You look good too." I allow my eyes to drop down his body. He's wearing dark jeans, stylish leather sneakers, a black sweater, and his baseball cap.

His mouth twitches at one corner, like he's not sure if he should smile or not. "Thank you. Should we head downstairs?"

"I'm ready. Let's get this over with, hunky bear." I loop my arm around his, taking full advantage of feeling up his bicep. I must be a little too obvious about it though, because he slowly swivels his head to look at me, the expression on his face a little confused. He's likely wondering why I've gone the past six years barely noticing the way he looks and now I'm suddenly groping his muscles every chance I get.

My brain is mush. Is this just confusion from the whole fake dating situation, or have I developed a serious attraction to my best friend?

I'm the last one to slide into the limo that will be chauffeuring us around for the night. First, we have an hour drive into the larger town that has the fancier restaurants and wineries. The only options here are mom and pop cafes, which are delicious, but not up to snuff for Mildred's bachelorette party ... or so she thinks.

All the girls are dressed similarly to myself: sexy but warm ... except for Trudy. She's going to freeze her tuchus off in her tiny, revealing dress and strappy stilettos.

I look at my sister and raise a brow in question, but she just shrugs and looks grumpily at Trudy.

"Um, Trudy," I place a hand on her very bare knee. "Did you bring a coat or anything? I think we're supposed to get more snow this evening."

Trudy giggles. "Girl, I'm from Kansas." She waves me off good humoredly. "I'll be fine!"

"Okay, if you're sure," I say. But I really want to tell her Central Kansas winters are a lot different than Vermont winters.

Mildred nods to the driver and he pulls out onto the road and rolls up the window separating us from him. The other two bridesmaids (Kelseigh and Presleigh? I can't remember) pop open a bottle of champagne. Everyone squeals when it explodes all over the place, not caring that this particular bottle of champagne was probably two-hundred dollars.

Glasses are filled and passed around. I guzzle mine quickly, enjoying the way it burns my throat and makes me feel warm and relaxed. I look over at Trudy. She's googling the champagne brand. I can tell when she finds the price, because I hear her gasp.

Music starts playing loudly from the speakers and everyone dances in their seats. I'm going to need several more glasses of champagne at this rate.

Normally, I'm all for having fun. But while sitting next to the woman my ex cheated on me with and putting on a happy face for the sister who hid important information from me ... it's a challenge to be in a party mood.

A second bottle of champagne is soon popped and poured with only slightly less fanfare than the first. Mildred quickly drains her glass and I make a mental note to watch her tonight. I don't want her to feel like crap on her wedding day.

"So, Trudy," Mildred says, using the remote to turn the music down slightly. "How did you meet Todd?"

I widen my eyes in warning, but Mildred ignores me.

Trudy sighs dreamily. "I started cutting his hair two months ago! We've been inseparable ever since."

My stomach rolls, making me wish I hadn't drunk that glass of champagne. I don't want Todd back, I really don't. But the knowledge that he cared so little for me after all those years together definitely stings.

"I still can't get over that amazing head of dark hair he has!" She sighs again and sips her champagne.

Mildred nods in acquiesce. "Ahh, so you were the other woman for several months then?"

Trudy's eyebrows draw together in confusion. "What?"

"Mildred," I say in a warning tone. "Enough."

"My sister has been dating Todd for seven years. And just recently broke up with him when she found your note on his car." Mildred pours herself another glass with a smug smile on her face.

Trudy looks at me with a horrified expression. "You're kidding! Oh my gosh." Her eyebrows draw together slightly, like she's deep in thought. "But I've never left a note on Todd's car. He's weirdly protective of that thing."

I look at my sister, who's wearing the same confused expression that I am. "Really?" I ask, and Trudy nods. She has no reason to lie about it, but I have to wonder where the note came from.

"Molly, I'm really sorry. I had no idea! There weren't any signs of him having a girlfriend."

"It's okay. You didn't know," I tell her, trying not to let this get out of hand and ruin the evening. "It was for the best that we ended things, anyway."

She looks down intently at her champagne. "You're not just saying that to throw me off because you secretly want him?"

I scoff. "Um, no. He's all yours."

"Are you sure? Because I'd totally trade for that hunk of man meat you're currently with."

I withhold an eye roll. She and Todd are made for each other, clearly. "I'm sure."

Chapter 24

Brooks

Once we finally arrive at some kind of luxurious gentlemen's club in the city, I'm ready to get out of Preston's Land Rover. I somehow ended up right next to Todd, and it's taken all of my self control not to put him in a headlock just because I can. *And* because he's a horrible person.

Todd sneers at me before exiting the vehicle and loudly asking Preston, "Are you sure they'll even allow him inside dressed like *that*?"

"Oh, get over yourself. He looks fine," Preston says in an annoyed tone.

There are two groomsmen besides Todd who rode here with us. One, Charles, is a friend of Preston's from college, who actually seems like a decent guy. And the other is Preston's younger brother, Kenneth, who looks barely twenty-one. They're all dressed in slacks, button-down shirts, and loafers or Oxford shoes. I'm the only one wearing jeans ... and definitely the only one who even owns a baseball cap, let alone wore one tonight.

A middle-aged, but pretty brunette meets us at the front door and greets Preston like an old friend, offering a kiss on each cheek. She leads us to a private dressing room where five red velvet robes are hanging in separate locker type nooks.

"Okay, gentlemen, the purpose of The Lounge is to provide a deluxe rejuvenating evening. For utmost comfort, we recommend undressing down to your undergarments and wearing the robes."

She nods and leaves us in the dressing room. I glance around the room, taking in all the polished, dark wood and the fireplace roaring along the far wall. Oddly enough, it reminds me of my parents' house.

We begin undressing when I hear a low whistle from behind me. "Damn. How do I get muscles like that?"

I glance over my shoulder to see Preston's younger brother ogling me unashamedly.

"Right?" Preston says with a laugh.

Todd huffs an irritated breath out through his nose. "I guess some people are into the whole meathead thing."

Charles chuckles. "Sounds like someone's a little jealous."

Todd's mouth twists in disgust. "Am not," he mutters under his breath, throwing the robe over his slim body.

Poor guy was probably freezing with so little meat on his bones. I pretend to ignore their chatter, although it is a bit amusing. I wish they could see Drew. They'd develop some serious muscle-envy. Even *I* have a bit of a man-crush on my brother-in-law.

I put my own robe on and turn to see Preston squeezing his arm where a bicep should be. His lips turn down slightly in a frown. "I really should've worked out leading up to the wedding."

"It's a little late now, man," Charles tells him with a smack on the back. The slap on his bare skin making us all wince.

"Ow!" He steps away from Charles. "I *know* it's too late now."

Kenneth snickers. "You worried Mildred won't be happy with what she sees on the wedding night?"

Preston puffs out his chest. "Oh, she'll have *plenty* to be pleased about tomorrow night." He raises his eyebrows up and down suggestively.

Kenneth rolls his eyes. "You don't have to lie to me. We used to share a room."

Preston grabs a hand towel from his cubby and begins snapping his little brother with it. A knock comes from the door and everyone straightens up. Preston throws his robe on and answers the door.

The same brunette from earlier is standing there. "Are you gentlemen ready to head to the smoke room?"

"Absolutely," Preston answers.

The five of us quickly slide on the red slippers that match our robes and follow the woman to a large, private room. It looks similar to the dressing room, but more formal. Five, leather wing-back chairs are arranged in front of the fireplace with a large selection of bourbons and Cuban cigars on a cart in front of them.

Personally, I never understood the whole cigar thing. So I opt for some fine bourbon instead. The rest of the guys select their cigars and we sit in the chairs and relax. I'm shocked by how much I'm enjoying myself. This is a surprisingly normal bachelor party.

Until ...

Bohemian music begins playing loudly through some speakers near the fireplace, and three belly dancers enter the room. Todd and Kenneth grin conspiratorially and Preston glares at them.

"Are you guys serious right now?" he whispers through gritted teeth.

"You said no strippers, and they're *not* strippers," Todd whispers back, Kenneth nodding enthusiastically beside him.

Preston rolls his eyes and gives the ladies a polite smile. I'll give Preston credit; he completely focuses on his cigar and keeps his eyes steered clear of the belly dancers. I'm not interested in watching them either … Apparently, when you have a Vanderbilt girl waiting for you back home, belly dancers just don't hold the same temptation. Preston glances at me and I silently raise my glass to him. He raises his glass too, then takes a sip.

Fifteen minutes later, the dancers wrap up and leave the room.

Preston turns an irritated gaze on his cousin and brother. "I didn't realize I had to specify no scantily clad women of any kind."

"You're no fun," Todd says, rolling his eyes and relaxing back in his chair.

"Someday, cousin, you'll be so in love with someone you won't even want to look at another woman."

Todd scoffs. "That ship has sailed. The only girl I ever loved is with someone else now." He gives me a knowing look.

Preston sits forward in his chair. "Really? If you loved Molly, you would've treated her better."

"Human beings weren't meant to be monogamous," Todd says with a shrug. "The divorce rate wouldn't be so high if people realized that."

"You're despicable. How are we related?" Preston's nose scrunches up in disgust. "You never deserved Molly."

My fists clench at the smirk on Todd's smug face. He's not even remotely apologetic for hurting her, which makes me want to hurt *him*. I remind myself he's not even worth the effort. But my hand grows tighter around the glass in my hand.

"Pretty sure it's the other way around. I was doing her a favor," Todd retorts, staring at me with a look of defiance.

The sound of glass breaking and clattering to the ground along with a small splash of liquid jars us and we all look around the room. I'm as surprised as them to notice it was my glass of bourbon. That I apparently smashed in my own fist. Oops.

Looking down at my hand, I see a spot of blood where a shard of glass nicked my palm.

Preston stands. "Come on, Brooks. Let's get that cleaned up. This room is feeling a little stuffy anyway." He glares at Todd.

I'm liking Preston more and more all the time.

After sleeping like the dead, my body has a hard time waking up the next morning. I can feel cool air on one of my legs, indicating I have one leg outside the covers. Despite only being half covered with blankets, I feel surprisingly hot. Which seems weird since the temperature probably dropped below freezing last night. When I feel something tickling my chest, my eyes fly open and I'm ready to smack the spider or whatever it is on me.

But instead I find Molly's head on my chest, and one of her arms thrown over my bare torso. When I went to bed after the bachelor party last night, she wasn't back yet. She must've slipped into bed like a ninja.

Her body heat explains why I'm so warm. But seeing her snuggled up against me sends warmth through my insides as well. My throat thickens with a rush of emotion I wasn't expecting ... probably because I've pictured this exact scenario so many times. But when I pictured it, we were a real couple. Not a fake one.

I swallow the thickness in my throat and try to hold still so she can sleep. I relax and decide to just enjoy the feeling of having her cuddled up in bed with me. Is it wrong to not wake her and put some distance between us? I'm not sure. All I know is it feels really nice.

And she must think so too, since she's sound asleep. Or maybe she's dreaming about Todd and she thinks I'm him. My eyebrows draw together at the thought, and my body stirs restlessly.

The movement wakes Molly, who doesn't seem to know what's happening at first. I feel her eyelashes flutter open against my chest and she releases a sleepy sigh. I wait for her realization and it doesn't even take a full second before her head pops up and her wide, horrified eyes meet mine.

I smile at her. "Well, good morning."

She gasps and jumps up to her knees before flying off the bed. "Why didn't you wake me? Or shove me off of you?" she asks breathlessly.

It's hard to repress my smile at the sight of her ... hair askew, bangs flipping up on each side, a red splotch on her face where her cheek was against my chest. And her pajama top that came unbuttoned on the bottom, showing off her very nice belly button.

"You looked so peaceful. I felt bad waking you," I tell her with a shrug and an apologetic smile. "Next time, I'll shove you off the bed. I promise."

I definitely won't do that ... not when I enjoyed it so much, but I'm not telling Molly that.

She finally looks down at her pajamas, possibly feeling cold air on her stomach, and gasps again. "Brooks! Tell me next time I'm indecent! Oh my gosh."

Molly runs into that bathroom, closing the door and locking it behind her. I finally release the laugh I've been holding in.

"I heard that!" she yells on the other side of the bathroom door.

Chapter 25

Molly

Brooks was already asleep when I got back from the bachelorette party last night. I was exhausted from keeping my sister out of trouble while winery hopping, and crawled right into bed without even showering.

Looking in the bathroom mirror, my face flushes all over again. My hair is a mess, and my belly button is showing! Ugh.

Waking up nestled against Brooks was warm and oh so sweet, until my brain caught up with my body and reminded me we're *not* a couple, and we *don't* snuggle. Through the bathroom window, I can see a fresh blanket of snow coating the back patio outside. Ah, the air was probably extra cold last night, so, naturally, I cozied with my handsome heater.

Well, not *my* handsome heater. But *a* handsome heater. I was asleep. It was a survival instinct!

I briefly think back to the sight I woke up to. Brooks with sleepy eyes, warm skin, and that disheveled blonde hair. Also, I think his arms were inside his unicorn onesie, but his legs weren't. I laugh at the thought of him half in and half out of the onesie, with one bare leg on top of the covers. He must've been burning up last night with me crowding him like that.

Dragging my hands down my face, I groan once more at my embarrassment. Then I make myself get in the shower and try to recover this day, hopefully with my dignity still intact.

I shower and blow dry my hair before rushing to the walk-in closet, still trying to avoid Brooks' eyes.

Selecting a simple button-down shirt and some leggings, I get dressed. Then with a deep breath, I force myself to open the closet door and forget about the snuggling ordeal.

Brooks is sitting on the bed, looking completely unembarrassed and unaffected. Cool as a cucumber. He smiles at me and I take him in for a moment before noticing his hand has a bandage wrapped around it. My eyes widen, and Brooks notices what I'm looking at. He attempts to hide his bandaged hand behind his back.

Worried, I rush toward him and pull his arm out from its hiding spot. I take his hand in mine and examine it.

He flinches and draws his hand back. "Ow!"

"What happened to your hand?" I ask, my voice raised with alarm.

He holds his hand and winces, then tries to disguise the wince as a smirk. "So, how'd you sleep last night, cuddle bug?" he asks with fake cheeriness.

"Tell me what happened last night."

Brooks casually lifts himself off the bed. "It's nothing. Aren't you going to be late for hair and makeup?"

I tap my foot on the floor impatiently. "Tell me what happened to your hand."

"It's really not a big deal," he explains, feigning nonchalance. "Just boys being boys." Brooks walks toward the bathroom and I follow him closely.

I pin him with an exasperated look. "Did you guys wrestle bears or something?"

His eyebrows shoot up. "That was an option? Vermont is wild."

"Brooks," I warn.

He sighs in defeat. "I accidentally smashed the glass I was holding, and cut my hand," he says before rushing into the bathroom, closing the door and locking it.

"*Accidentally*? How do you accidentally smash a glass?" I demand.

"Sorry, can't hear you!" he yells from the other side of the door.

I glance at the clock on my nightstand. I only have five minutes until I'm expected for the bridal breakfast. "I have to go ... but tonight, you're giving me more details."

I hear a quiet chuckle from the other side of the door. I think we both realize I'll be way too exhausted tonight to even remember this conversation. Mildred and Preston's wedding ceremony doesn't start until six, and my perfectionist mother and sister have us booked up all day for hair, makeup, and photos.

After sitting in a chair for four hours getting primped (yes, *four*), the makeup artist finally puts the final touches on my face. Standing from my seat, I yawn and stretch my back. My mother looks at me disapprovingly. Avoiding her gaze, I turn and grab my dress from the rack. There's a curtained area set up for privacy, so I duck behind it and put my dress on.

A knock comes from the door of the large bedroom we've taken over for the day. Curious, I leave my hiding spot and go back to stand next to my sister. My mother opens the door to find Harold there. He nods toward me and hands her a small red package, wrapped up with a white bow.

My spine stiffens, already knowing what's inside the package. The antique spoons are always wrapped the same. But why is Todd still sending them to me? I wish he'd stop already.

My mother takes the box and dismisses Harold, then strides toward me and gives me the box.

I don't meet her gaze when I take the box from her. Instead, I turn my attention to my gorgeous sister, who's still getting her makeup perfected. "How are you, Mildred? Can I do anything?" I ask, trying to turn all the attention back on the bride.

She smirks. "Yeah, you can. Open the mysterious box that was just delivered."

I inhale a deep breath and blow it out slowly. "Fine."

Untying the white bow, I glance at my mother, who's watching closely. I wonder if she knows Todd sends me these packages ... I wonder if she's a conspirator. I open the box and, unsurprisingly, there's a gorgeous antique spoon inside. This one has the initials M.W. etched on the handle. I can't help but imagine what the spoon's story could be.

There's a note tucked inside the box, and I pull it out, angling my body so no one else can read it over my shoulder.

Molly,

I have no doubt you'll look absolutely perfect today. You always do ... whether it's a formal bridesmaid's dress, or a potato sack. Doesn't matter. You'll look incredible.

-Your secret admirer

I withhold an eye roll. Todd should really consider sending notes like this to Trudy instead of me. She's the one here with him. I have no interest in his attention any longer.

"Well?" my mother asks. "What does the note say? Who's it from?" She shifts her weight from one stilettoed foot to the other.

Studying her face for a moment, I try to decipher if she's playing dumb, or if she really doesn't know. But her expression doesn't give anything away.

I shrug and hand her the note. "My secret admirer."

Her eyes flit around the note, reading it quickly. "How curious."

"How romantic!" Mildred exclaims, grabbing the note from our mother and reading it for herself. The other two bridesmaids rush over and read it too. "You don't think it's from Brooks?" Mildred asks before handing the note back to me.

I shake my head. "I don't think so. I've been receiving the spoons since before we started dating."

"Maybe they're from Todd?" my mother asks, her eyes twinkling like the idea delights her. As if a spoon and a simple note could erase how he's treated me.

Shrugging, I place my hands on Mildred's slim shoulders. "Enough about the dumb note. Let's focus on the *real* romance happening today."

Mildred looks up at me, beaming happily.

I walk down to the living room where the wedding party is taking photos. Mildred and Preston went down ahead of the bridesmaids and groomsmen to have their own special moment before the ceremony. Mildred didn't care as much about the tradition of a groom not seeing his bride until she walks down the aisle as she did about having the best lighting for photos.

The multiple wedding planners have decorated the cabin so thoroughly, it barely resembles a cabin any longer. It looks more like the Palace of Versailles than a cabin. Gold sconces with LED candles are hung along the banisters, intertwined with fresh greenery and white roses. It's gorgeous, just not as earthy and rustic as I pictured for a snowy cabin wedding.

There's not a table or banister left undecorated. The rustic, albeit classy cabin has been transformed into a field of flowers. (With gold and diamonds sprinkled in.)

The fireplace is the centerpiece for the ceremony, and it's been decked out with flowers and greenery as well as a hand painted sign hung above the mantle that says "Preston & Mildred Annelise" in a scrolly calligraphy font.

My sister and her groom look picture-perfect standing in front of the fireplace, grinning at each other happily.

One of the other bridesmaids (McKenzeigh?) gasps. "Oh Mildred, it's absolutely breathtaking!" The other blonde agrees with her.

"Thank you! I love it," she responds, barely taking her eyes off of Preston.

Todd, Kenneth, and Preston's friend from college enter the room from the opposite side of the house where they've been getting ready.

Todd's eyes widen when he sees me, then they slowly move down the length of my body. The old Molly probably would've been flattered to get this attention from him, but now I just find it creepy.

I mean, he literally has a gorgeous date here with him. Someone who, just a few weeks ago, he thought was more fun to be with than me. I wonder once more where that mysterious note on Todd's car came from. If Trudy didn't write it, who did?

Shaking the thought, I decide to figure it out another day. I walk toward my sister, making sure to ignore Todd. Which is exactly what I plan to do all day.

Ignoring him up to this point really hasn't been difficult since I have Brooks here with me: someone I genuinely enjoy being around. I've even been looking forward to going to bed each night. Not that I'd admit that to anyone. Ever.

Especially not Hope and Layla.

"You guys look amazing," I tell Mildred and Preston, giving them each a big hug. "And the decorators did a great job."

"Thank you, Molly." Mildred looks at me with teary eyes, making me wonder if she's still feeling bad about withholding the information about Todd's trust fund. But it could also be because it's her wedding day. Probably the latter.

Preston leans his head down. "How's Brooks's hand?" His voice is just low enough for me and Mildred to hear.

I decide to act like I know what happened, hoping he'll give me more details.

I frown. "He's okay. His hand is still in pain from the glass."

Preston's jaw moves from side to side like he's grinding his teeth. "I wish he would've taken his anger out on Todd instead of his bourbon glass." His eyes shift to Todd briefly. "What a waste of good bourbon."

"Yeah." I purse my lips as if I know what he's talking about. "I can't believe Todd was being such a jerk."

"Well, I think he got his point across by smashing a glass with his fist."

I nod. "And ... what point would that be?"

"Not to say anything disrespectful about his woman," he says with a smirk, like it was so obvious.

"Right." I huff out a little laugh. "Brooks will whoop his butt next time for sure."

A man and a woman enter the room. They're dressed in black pants and white button-down shirts, and they're carrying cameras and large bags, which I assume are filled with lenses and such.

They get right to work telling us where to stand and setting up their equipment, but it's all a blur. All I can do is picture Brooks trying so hard to control his temper about whatever Todd said that he shattered his glass.

The fact that someone would have that kind of reaction to another person disrespecting me gives me that strange fuzzy feeling in my stomach, and makes me feel warm all over.

I don't even care what Todd said. I only care about the man I woke up next to this morning. The same one wearing a unicorn onesie and goofy underwear. The same one who defended my honor without saying a word.

I'm beginning to dread heading back to Kansas ... but only because I have a very strong feeling I'm gonna miss waking up next to Brooks Windell every morning.

Thirty minutes before the wedding ceremony, I'm in the designated bridal party room helping my sister go to the bathroom one last time before walking down the aisle. This is something they don't warn you about before committing to be someone's maid of honor. Bridal bathroom duty. It's like babysitting a toddler in taffeta.

Mildred looks at me with an unamused smile as she washes her hands. "Thanks, sis. Let's hope this is the last time ever that you'll have to help me in the bathroom."

I close my eyes and cross my fingers, making her laugh.

When I look at her again, she's looking back at me in the bathroom mirror. Her expression is serious, and she opens her mouth to speak then closes it again.

"What is it?" I ask. She looks nervous and unsure then turns to dry her hands on the bathroom towel. "If you want out of this, it's not too late. I'll help you climb down the banister."

She chuckles. "Are you kidding? I couldn't last a day without Preston." She sighs and glances at the door. "It's just, I think Todd's mom and ours are ..."

She stops suddenly when our mother opens the bathroom door and steps inside. She notices our silence upon her entering and looks from me to Mildred and back skeptically.

"Molly, sweetheart," she finally says. "We need you."

I look at my sister, but her eyes are scanning the floor. "Okay, sure. What for?"

"Umm. Your father," She pauses. "He needs help with his tie."

Neither my mom nor Mildred will look me directly in the eye. I'm not sure what's going on, but my father has never in his life had trouble tying a tie.

"Uh, okay," I say.

My mother opens the door and lets me walk through before she follows. There's a strange sensation in the pit of my stomach warning me that I'm being led to the gallows, or something just as bad.

We walk out of the bridal room and down the upstairs hallway in silence before she stops in front of her and my father's bedroom door. She feigns a smile before gesturing toward the door, then turning and walking away.

"Weddings make people weird," I mutter to myself as I open the door and step inside.

The room is eerily quiet. "Dad?" I call out.

Someone who's not my father appears from the small nook off of their room, which they turned into a library. Actually, it's someone I'd rather not be alone with at all.

I cross my arms, trying to look intimidating and irritated. "Todd, what are you doing in here?"

"Molls, thanks for coming," he says with a confident grin.

The nickname he's always used for me causes me to bristle. "I came to help my father, and since he's not even here, I'm leaving." I turn and stride toward the door but he catches my arm before I reach the handle.

"Please, I want to show you something. Then you're free to go." He lets go of my arm.

I contemplate for a moment and decide I'll see what it is he wants. Then I can leave with little to no drama. "Fine. But make it quick."

He places his hand on my back and guides me toward the library. His hand feels cold and foreign on my bare skin. Nothing like Brooks's warm, calloused hand that simultaneously heightens my heart rate, and then calms it again.

Todd leads me inside the small space and my eyes widen in surprise. The room is dark and dim except for tea candles placed all over the bookshelves. Red rose petals are scattered all over the floor as if a Valentine's Day bouquet was annihilated here. The flickering candles cast shadows on Todd's face, making him look sinister.

"This seems like a fire hazard," I say, wishing Brooks was here to laugh about it with me.

Todd groans irritably. "You're not going to make this easy, are you?"

"Huh?" I ask, confused at his remark. To my absolute horror, the man in front of me, the one I'm no longer dating, drops down on one knee. I can feel the blood drain from my face when he pulls a velvet box out of his tuxedo pocket, an arrogant grin on his face the whole time.

I can feel my face twitching as if it doesn't know what to do. A corner of my mouth pulls up, wanting to laugh. But my eyebrows draw together in annoyance. But also, my eyes are filling with hot, angry tears. Pick an emotion already, Molly!

Todd translates my horrified expression as the sign to continue and opens the ring box where an ostentatious diamond ring is nestled in white silk. The ring is huge and has a modern design. Absolutely not what I would ever choose.

"I'm sorry it's taken me so long. But you're the one for me. Marry me, Molls," he says it as a statement, not a question.

"Todd, stop." I walk over to the bookshelves and start blowing out the tea candles. Because when I flee from this room, I don't want to worry about a fire burning the entire cabin down.

"What are you doing?" He stands and walks over to me, shooing me away from the candles.

"This is literally so dangerous. Candles right next to paperbacks? No."

"Stop talking about the damned candles!" he demands, his voice angry. "I just asked you to marry me, which is what *you've* always dreamed of. Now answer me." He wraps his arms around my waist and presses me against him. I squirm and try to get away but he's not relenting.

"Let me go! I don't want to marry you!"

My words must surprise him because he gasps and his hold on me loosens. I swat his hands away.

"I know you're only asking because you want your trust fund. But even if that weren't the case ... We're not right for each other. We never were."

"Who told you about the trust fund?" He has the audacity to sound offended.

"Does it really matter? You stayed with me because of money. I stayed with you to keep everyone happy. Everyone but myself." I shrug. "We both did this all wrong. Let's just move forward with our lives ... separately"

He scoffs, his face turning into a scowl. "Is this because of Brooks?"

A strangled sound comes out of my mouth. Something like a half laugh, half groan. "This has nothing to do with Brooks." I rub my temples with my index fingers. "I don't want to marry you because of ... well, *you*."

His jaw drops.

I laugh, but there's no humor in it, and I blow out the rest of the candles while he stands there looking baffled. "Look at the ring, for instance." I gesture to the obnoxious diamond. "You obviously don't know me at all."

His jaw tenses. "Do you have any idea how much this ring cost?" He kicks the pile of roses at his feet.

"That's not the point." I sigh and take a step toward the door. "After seven years, you don't even know what I like." Smiling sympathetically, I continue, "Except the spoons. The spoons and romantic notes you sent always gave me faith in us ... but I need more than spoons."

He shifts on his feet and rests a hand on his narrow hip. "Molly, what the hell are you talking about?"

"The antique spoons you send me," I say, holding my hands out like that will jog his memory. "You just sent me one this morning."

"Sorry to continually disappoint you, but I've never sent you a spoon." He looks down at his feet, shaking his head. "You're so freaking blind."

"What's that supposed to mean?" As soon as the words are out of my mouth, I remember Hope and Layla asking me if Brooks could be the one sending the spoons.

My cheeks heat and my heart flutters as I think back over the years to all of the beautiful spoons paired with romantic notes. But why would he be the one sending them? All these years ...

"Our parents are going to be pissed at you for denying my proposal, by the way. They set this whole thing up." He rolls his eyes.

"And you went along with it?" I manage to choke out, despite my thoughts still swirling about Brooks. "Why don't you propose to Trudy instead? You remember her? Your *date*. Just relight the candles and I'll send her on up."

He smirks. "Trudy isn't marriage material. And my parents offered her a thousand dollars this morning if she'd take the first flight back to Kansas. She was on a plane an hour later."

I snort. "Classy." Glancing at the grandfather clock next to my parents' bed, I move toward the door again. "We really need to go. The wedding is about to start."

Chapter 26

Brooks

Sitting in my designated seat in the living room-turned-wedding ceremony, I can't stop craning my head and looking over my shoulder. Molly said she'd meet me at our room before the wedding so we could walk down together, but she never showed.

I'm assuming she just got busy helping her sister or something, but I can't stop worrying that it was something more. I waited for her until the last possible second before I headed downstairs on my own.

The tiny orchestra assembled at the side of the large living area begins to play elegant music, and Preston appears at the foot of the grand staircase along with his parents and the Vanderbilts. He ushers both sets of parents to their seats in the front rows before taking his place next to the officiant. He has a huge grin on his face, as every groom should.

The music changes and the bridesmaids and grooms-men appear, first Charles and one of the blondes, then Kenneth and the other blonde. Lastly, Molly and Todd come into view. I peruse her slowly from top to bottom. I'm her fake boyfriend after all; what boyfriend wouldn't appreciate his girl in that dress?

Her dark hair is piled up on top of her head in a twisty updo, and her bangs are pinned to the side with a sparkly pin. The red, silky dress drapes over her body to perfection, like it was poured onto her. It takes everything inside of me not to gape and drool. I've seen Molly dressed up, and dressed down. But that dress was made for her. It fits her hot little body perfectly.

How could her mother not see how gorgeous she is?

As Molly draws nearer to me, her eyes meet mine. I wink at her playfully, but her expression stays serious. She looks as if she's seen a ghost, which makes me even more worried about what kept her from meeting me earlier. Todd is stiff next to her and looks grouchy. Like the other bridesmaids and groomsmen, their arms are linked together as they walk. But they look really awkward, like they're trying to touch each other as little as possible.

Fine by me.

When they pass by me, I get a view of the back of the dress. I nearly fall to my knees, my legs feeling suddenly weak. I didn't think it could get any better until I saw the back. She really does have an excellent butt. I wasn't making that up. I'll have to remind her later.

The music changes again, this time louder and more serious. Mr. and Mrs. Vanderbilt stand and everyone else follows suit. Mildred makes an appearance at the top of the steps, and glides down them slowly, obvious-ly soaking up the attention of her grand entrance.

While everyone is staring awestruck at the bride. I turn and gaze at Molly again. She looks back at me, her eyes looking teary like she might cry at any second. I give her a reassuring smile, but her serious expression doesn't change. The way she's looking at me makes me feel vulnerable, stripped down, naked. Like she's looking straight through me. Through the jokes, and the playboy facade.

Like she's really seeing me for the first time.

Mildred finishes her bridal entrance, and Molly's at-tention turns toward her sister.

For the rest of the ceremony, all I can do is wonder why Molly was looking at me like that, and why she's never looked at me that way before.

After the vows are said and Mildred is wifed-up, we're ushered out row by row. It doesn't take long since there are probably around seventy-five guests, if I had to guess. We're herded into the large dining room, which is now lined with standing tables for a cocktail and hors d'oeuvres hour. With the large table removed, the room actually feels quite large.

I make polite small talk while I wait for the wedding party to get done taking photos. I've been a wedding date too many times to count. And I've always thought I was a fantastic wedding date ... but I've never been the date of someone *in* the wedding. And let me tell you, it's a lonely date indeed. The date of the maid-of-honor.

I sigh and take a drink of my hot-pink cocktail that they're calling *The Mildred*. It's a little sweet for me; I should've gotten *The Preston* instead.

Just as the cocktail hour is almost up, Molly walks, no, floats, into the dining room. Every man in the room looks up from his drink as she walks across the room toward me, but she doesn't notice.

"Brooks, I'm so sorry I didn't meet you before the wedding," she says, sounding slightly out of breath.

I take a step closer to her, unable to help myself. The red dress calls to me like a bull being confronted by a matador. "That's all right." I smile. "Is everything okay?"

She hesitates, her eyes meeting mine and not wavering. The same look she gave me during the wedding. "It's been an informative day."

I quirk a brow, but she doesn't offer any more details. Instead, she takes the cocktail glass out of my hand and drains the rest of my drink in one big gulp.

Her shoulders seem to relax a bit. "You look really good," she says, finally smiling a little as she peruses my black trousers, velvet loafers, matching velvet vest, and red and black plaid bow tie.

I look her over the same way and whistle low and slow. "I don't look half as sexy as you. Harold almost had to come sweep me up off the floor after I saw you in that dress."

Instead of brushing off my compliment and rolling her eyes like she normally does ... she blushes. A deep, pink blush that starts at her shoulders and goes all the way up to her bangs.

I decide I love seeing Molly blush, so I continue. "I mean, that dip in the fabric that shows off your back? And the way it clings to your very good butt?" I close my eyes and blow out a breath. "Lord have mercy."

She leans toward me and whispers my name, "Brooks. We need to talk."

Cocking my head to the side, I study her. Did I go too far with the compliments? She's still blushing, but I thought that was a good sign.

"The cocktail hour has come to an end, and you're welcome to continue the celebration in the reception area," Harold announces from the doorway.

As the guests start shuffling toward the door, I notice Molly's and Todd's mothers glaring at me from the doorway.

Molly sighs in frustration. "I'm sorry, I have to get to the head table with the rest of the wedding party. I'll find you as soon as I can, okay?"

Steadying myself, I try my hardest not to allow my shoulders to droop or give away my disappointment that she can't spend more time with me. But today isn't about me— it's Preston and Mildred's day.

"Sure, okay." I grab her hand and squeeze it gently. She gives me a hesitant smile back and scurries off toward the door, seemingly ignoring the narrow-eyed glare her mother is giving her.

What did I miss today?

Chapter 27

Molly

Here I was, worried that Todd's abrupt proposal would cause me to be distracted from the wedding. Well, I haven't thought of my ex-boyfriend once. Nope. Instead, I was distracted throughout the ceremony—and *more* wedding photos—with a steady stream of memories. Analyzing my friendship with Brooks over the past six years. Wondering why he'd send those romantic notes along with the spoons. And contemplating if he meant them, or if they were just to give me a confidence boost when life was difficult.

And if he did mean them, if he's had feelings for me all this time, what do I do with that information?

My head fills with thoughts of him being there for me, and never judging me when I needed to rant. Or when I listened to whatever music I enjoy, or bought the house I really wanted. He has supported me through it all. And believed in me enough to start a business together.

And then there's the mysterious flutters that keep happening around him. Are those friendly flutters? Or more?

I know the answer to that one. Especially after my dream a few nights ago, featuring Brooks the sexy Viking fearlessly leading a ship through the Netherlands to conquer something. I don't know if Vikings really used to sail shirtless, with rippling muscles and a gentle breeze blowing through their blonde locks, but that's definitely how my dream represented them.

I sigh, wishing I could talk this out with Brooks. To sit next to him, inhaling his manly scent, watching the vein that pulses in his muscular neck, and enjoying his small, flirtatious touches that make my entire body sizzle.

I push my meal around my plate with a fork.

"Everything okay?" Mildred asks from where she's sitting next to me.

Forcing a smile on my face, I sit up straighter. "Yeah, of course! Today went perfectly."

She grins. "It really did! Isn't it crazy how they transformed this room so fast?"

I look around the living room that went from ceremony to reception area in one hour flat. Impressive for sure. The room is now filled with round tables, red tablecloths, and gorgeous floral centerpieces. There's even an awning at the entrance decorated from top to bottom with mistletoe.

"Yeah, I can't believe they got this all done in an hour."

Preston drapes his arm around my sister and leans in. "Where'd Brooks go?"

My head whips up and searches the room. He's no longer seated at one of the round tables with the other guests. I was too busy with my own thoughts to notice that he left.

"I'm not sure?" I answer, shrugging and trying to look casual. But on the inside, I'm watching the clock and counting down the minutes until I can go find him.

The wedding planner comes over to our table and hands Todd a cordless microphone. I breathe a sigh of relief that it's finally time for the best man and maid of honor toasts.

After this, I can go in search of my date.

Todd stands and smiles at the crowd. I know him well enough to know it's a fake smile. I don't think he actually wanted to marry me, but his pride is hurt nonetheless.

"Good evening," he starts, and the room quiets down. "I'm Todd Du Pont, the groom's right-hand man." Whistles and cheers whoop through the crowd. "When Preston asked me to be his best man, I was truly honored. We've always been more like best friends than cousins." Todd gives Preston a tight smile. I can't see

Preston's face, but I can picture him withholding an eye roll. "Watching Mildred and Preston fall in love has been like witnessing poetry in motion. Or a real-life Shakespearean play. It made me desire that kind of love for myself, something I thought would happen sooner rather than later." Todd shoots me an annoyed glance.

I grab my champagne flute and take a small sip, attempting to keep my expression neutral and not give away that I think the best man is an infuriating twat.

"But I digress. Preston and Mildred, congratulations. I wish you both a lifetime of happiness." He raises his glass in the air and more cheers ensue as he takes a sip and then sits back down.

Todd reaches behind the bride and groom to hand me the microphone for my turn. I quickly take it from him, careful not to brush his hand with mine, lest it give him any ideas I've changed my mind.

When I stand, I have a better view of the room, and scan it once more for a certain handsome blonde man that's usually the center of attention. Unable to find him, I roll into my speech.

"As most of you know, I'm Molly, the bride's little sister." A collective *awe* sounds from the crowd. "Mildred and I have had our fair share of squabbles and disagreements over the years." I place my hand on her shoulder and look at her. Her eyes fill with tears and she brings her hand up to cover mine. I know we're both remembering the confession in the hot tub the other night and the information she hid from me. But I want her to know I forgive her. "But at the end of the day our love for each other overpowered all of that." One lone tear streams down her face, and she gives me the tiniest nod of thanks.

"I've been around Preston and Mildred a lot over the years, and have been forced to watch them fawn all over each other." The crowd laughs, and so do my sister and her groom. "There's never been a doubt in my mind that theirs is a *true* love." I glance briefly at Todd, who's scowling down at his plate. "The kind of love we all long for and deserve." A few amens ring out from the crowd and a light applause. "You guys have a love worth fighting for." I raise my glass. "Here's to a lifetime of fighting for each other."

We all take a sip of our champagne, and Mildred stands up and embraces me. A few seconds later, I feel Preston's arms around the both of us in one big group hug.

Once the applause dies down, the wedding planner quickly grabs the happy couple for the cake cutting. Knowing this is my opportunity to sneak away, I skirt around the perimeter of the room until I'm through the mistletoe awning and looking around the hallway for Brooks.

Harold is making the rounds throughout the house, making sure nothing is amiss, when he notices me.

"Are you looking for a certain large blonde man?" There's a hint of a smile in his serious voice. Harold has always had a soft spot for me.

I look at him sheepishly. "Yes, I am. Have you seen him?"

He nods his head toward the small sitting room, smirks, then continues walking down the long hallway.

Wasting no time, I peek inside the sitting room. Ahh, so this is where they stuck the children of the guests. When I see a flurry of paper airplanes flit across the room, my eyes widen. The half-dozen or so children erupt into giggles and run to capture their paper airplanes. Brooks is at the far edge of the room, clearly the leader of the chaos.

His hair is rumpled and his cheeks are pink like he's been running around ... playing. I smile to myself. How did it take me this long to realize how breathtakingly adorable he is?

The oldest boy in the room, if we're not counting the giant blonde, is wearing the bow tie Brooks had on earlier. Another little boy is wearing the velvet vest, leaving Brooks in just his dress shirt and trousers. The dress shirt is now unbuttoned at the top and the shirt sleeves are rolled up to show off his impressive forearms and smattering of manly arm hair.

He looks even yummier than the wedding cake.

All the children line up once more on the far side of the room, paper airplanes in hand. Brooks counts to ten and they release them again. A little girl, who I'd guess is barely three, bursts into tears when she sees her airplane crash-landed at her feet, the front end crumpled and caved in.

"Hey now." Brooks kneels in front of her, tugging gently on one of her pigtails. "I bet we can fix it."

She wipes her tears on the sleeve of her fancy dress and smiles. Brooks stands and she grabs onto his hand before dragging him back toward the table that is covered in paper—remnants of their craft time.

I can't stop watching him interact with the kids. It's absolutely precious. And it reminds me of watching him with his nieces. Suddenly, the thought of Brooks as a dad pops into my head. He'd be a really great dad.

The door creaks when my foot accidentally bumps it and Brooks turns and sees me watching them.

He smiles. "Well, look who finally found the fun room."

The children laugh at his comment, except for the little girl still gripping Brooks's hand. She looks downright possessive as she scowls at me. It's really hard to take her seriously though with her little pigtails and fluffy, pink dress.

"I think I've been replaced," I tell him, my eyes shifting to the little girl.

He chuckles and looks down at her. "Alice, this is my date, Molly."

Her bottom lip sticks out in a pout before she says, "Hi."

"Nice to meet you, Alice. Do you mind if I steal this big guy for a dance?"

She scrunches her nose up. "Can you fix my airplane first?"

"Here," I say. "Let me fix it. I'm really good at paper airplanes."

Alice looks skeptical, but seems to approve of my design once I'm finished.

"Thanks for playing with me, guys. But I have to go now," Brooks says to the kids, sticking his hands in his pockets. "I have a surprise though."

He walks over to the coffee table where his laptop bag is, takes his computer out, and starts playing an old episode of *Ducktales*. The kids are thrilled and all crowd onto the sofa to watch.

Brooks slides his hand into mine and leads me out the door and into the quiet hallway. The warmth of his hand simultaneously making me feel calm, and sending a zing of attraction through my body. His nearness has all of my senses on high alert. The feel of his rough hand in mine ... of his arm brushing against the fabric of my dress. The scent of his masculine cologne ... a scent so familiar that I feel at home when I inhale it. The sight of my small hand intertwined with his manly one. It's all overwhelming, making me feel dizzy.

We continue walking until we arrive at the entrance of the reception. Brooks stops me with a tug on my hand before I can step inside the bustling room. "You said we needed to talk?"

I take a shaky breath, feeling suddenly nervous. "Oh, right," I say, shrugging. "It can wait." I turn and try to walk into the reception again, not ready to voice everything that has transpired today.

Brooks stays me again with his hand. His free hand comes up to my chin, forcing me to look at him. Since I'm wearing heels, my face is close to his. And it hits me just how much my best friend has changed over the years. He's no longer the boy with the dewy skin who flies by the seat of his pants and flirts with anything that breathes ... he's a man now. With stubble on his chin, and the beginning of laugh lines forming around his eyes and mouth. And a look in his eyes that tells me he'd carry the weight of the world for me if I simply asked him to.

"Talk to me, Molly," he urges, his forehead creasing with concern.

My mouth opens to speak, to tell him I know about the spoons, to ask him if he meant the words he wrote in the notes.

"Uh, looks like we have a couple under the mistletoe." Preston's voice comes through the speakers. Our heads snap up and we see Preston and Mildred eyeing us from the head table. Preston has the microphone and a big grin. "You know what that means."

Everyone attending the reception turns their attention toward us as our heads tilt upward to see we've been standing directly under the mistletoe-covered awning.

I laugh awkwardly. "It's okay, we said no kissing," I remind him, giving him an out. But deep inside, I'm longing for this man to kiss me. To see what it would be like.

His eyes don't stray from mine, his expression serious. "Do you want me to kiss you?"

"But our deal—" I start, but he cuts me off.

"Forget our deal. Do you *want* me to kiss you?" he says each word slowly, his eyes boring into mine, searching for desire, or maybe permission.

Hesitating for a split second, I decided to answer honestly. "Yes," I say, my voice sounding breathy and foreign to my own ears.

He doesn't waste any more time. Brooks leans down and his lips brush mine gently in a tender caress. His hand slides around my waist to the bare skin of my back, and he pulls me closer to him. My hands slide up his strong arms and then around the back of his neck.

The same neck I've noticed an embarrassing number of times the past few weeks. He's all hard lines and masculinity to my silky softness. The mixture causes a delicious combustion.

He tilts his head one way, and I tilt mine the other like we've done this a million times. His soft mouth moves over mine repeatedly until I'm overwhelmed with the taste of him. Brooks's lips taste like Hot Tamales: sweet, spicy, and a little unexpected. But perfect.

The whoops and hollers, whistles and laughter from the reception bring us back to reality. Brooks pulls back slightly to look at me before one side of his mouth turns up into his signature smirk, reminding me of the boy I met six years ago.

The flash of cameras makes us both squint. We look around to see the flash is coming from the wedding photographers, and Brooks's eyes widen slightly.

"The bet," I whisper. "Brooks, I'm so sorry."

He wrinkles his nose, but doesn't look upset. "It's okay. It was worth it."

Chapter 28

Brooks

C rap. I wonder how much I can offer the photographer to conveniently lose those photos.

I look at Molly and see a smile lighting up her face. The cameraman is instantly forgotten. David doesn't know the Vanderbilts, anyway. The chances of him seeing that photo are very slim.

And would I honestly do anything differently, even if I had remembered the photographers? Hell no.

Kissing Molly was exhilarating. Like when you've waited in line for hours to ride a roller coaster, and you finally get your turn. The wait makes the experience even more fun. Except this was *way* more satisfying than that.

The orchestra has now switched out to a DJ, which I'm pleasantly surprised about. I was worried I'd have to remember how to waltz from the dance lessons my mother made all of us take years ago. I take Molly's hand and lead her onto the dance floor.

The song being played is fun and upbeat, allowing Molly and I to have a little space between us as we dance our hearts out. She looked at me differently today, and when she told me she wanted me to kiss her, it felt real. But was it real? Or did she just want to save face in front of all these people? I wouldn't judge her for it … I mean, who wants their fake boyfriend to deny them a kiss under the mistletoe? Especially with an awaiting audience.

But I have to know what changed today, what shifted. And *why* do Mrs. Vanderbilt and Todd's mother keep glaring at me with murderous expressions? I've sniffed all my food and beverages this evening to see if I can detect any poison.

The song switches to a slow one, and all is forgotten as my arm slides around Molly's waist and pulls her into me. This right here? It feels so right. Her body against mine, her eyes piercing mine, her lips on mine.

I always knew this would happen … that if I got a taste of her, I would never be able to get enough.

Molly allows her head to rest against my chest, and I nearly melt into a puddle right on the dance floor.

I allow my fingertips to find her spine, her very bare spine, thanks to this incredible backless dress. Thank you, Mildred.

My fingertips start at her lower back and slowly caress all the way up to the nape of her neck. Her skin is so soft, just as soft and silky as her dress. Hope blooms in my chest when goosebumps appear on her back from my touch. Or maybe she's just cold?

I pull her in tighter, just in case. Wouldn't want her to be hypothermic or anything. Just doing my gentlemanly duty ... although my thoughts are currently very far from gentlemanly. And it's not because I haven't been on a date in a few months; it's because this is Molly. *The* Molly. Everything feels different with her. More real, more intense, more passionate.

More everything.

Everything I've waited for. Everything I hoped to feel for all those other girls, but never even came close to.

I feel like a moron for ever thinking I'd find another girl who made me feel the way Molly does. It was pointless. And how do I ever explain that to her? That I was a total boy-toy trying to get over her? It sounds so stupid.

I try to put these thoughts out of my head, and just soak up the feeling of this girl in my arms. Because I don't know what's real and what's fake anymore. All I know is if I only get one night of this, I want to remember every detail.

Resting my chin on top of her head, I allow my hand to drop back down her spine, enjoying the feel of her impossibly soft skin again. And wishing I had one of those journals that David and Drew swear by. Because I want to write this all down and read it over and over again later.

To remember the best night of my life.

Feeling an unimpressive shove at my back, my head jerks up. My first instinct is to protect Molly, so I wrap both of my arms around her before swiveling my head to see who just shoved me.

Todd is standing there, alone. His eyes filled with rage. I'm not sure where Trudy ran off to, but I haven't seen her all day.

"What's your problem?" I ask him in a low voice, attempting to sway with Molly in my arms so as not to draw attention to the debacle.

"*You* are my problem," he hisses.

I rear back, noting his blood-shot eyes and wobbly legs. "Are you drunk? Go to bed, man."

"I'm not going to bed without Molly. She's mine. Always has been, always will be," he slurs, then sways on his wobbly legs.

Thankfully, Preston and Kenneth notice the drama their cousin is causing and rush toward us. They each grab one of his arms carefully, trying not to upset him more.

"Hey, let's get you to bed, okay?" Preston asks him. He groans and allows his cousins to drag him off the dance floor.

Unfortunately, they weren't able to drag Todd away from us before he had created a spectacle. Everyone is staring at us, and this time it's not because they're cheering for us to kiss under the mistletoe.

Mr. Vanderbilt makes his way through the crowd and stops in front of us. "Listen, Brooks. You seem like a good kid ... but I think it's best if you leave as well," he says quietly.

"Dad," Molly says in a baffled voice. "Brooks didn't even do anything."

He sighs heavily and drags a hand through his hair. "I know. But Todd's mother, and your own ... don't see it that way."

I feel my eyebrows shoot up, but I can't help it. I'm even more confused than I've been all damn day.

"If Brooks leaves, I leave," Molly says, standing up straight and looking her father directly in the eyes.

His eyes widen, looking almost ... proud. Then he nods his head. "Goodnight to both of you then." Calmly, he turns and leaves us.

— ell —

When we arrive back at our room, I can tell Molly is exhausted. I hate that the evening ended this way when we were having such a great time together. She slumps down on the bed with a frustrated groan. I sit next to her and rub her shoulders for a moment.

"How about I make you a nice hot bath and you can relax for a while?"

She looks up at me with teary eyes. "Really?"

I nod.

"With the lavender vanilla bath salts?"

"Whatever you want," I say, meaning it.

A tear slips down her cheek. "That sounds perfect." She sighs. "And afterward, we'll talk. I promise."

Swiping the tear off of her cheek with my thumb, I whisper, "All right." I give her a reassuring smile before turning and heading toward the bathroom to get her bath ready.

Maybe I should try to relax while she's in the tub... because my stomach is in knots, and my brain is fuzzy with anxious thoughts. Something shifted today, and I think it's good. But if I read her all wrong, I'll be wrecked.

Molly Vanderbilt is *it* for me. There's no one else.

My only other future is being a single, crazy cat man. Or maybe I'll have a herd of emotional-support Highland cows?

While Molly is in the bath, I change into my unicorn onesie and relax on the bed while watching funny animal videos on the internet. Funny animals always calm my brain.

When she finally steps out of the bathroom, her skin is pink from the hot water and she's wearing knee-high fuzzy socks with flannel shorts and a matching flannel top. Her hair has gone from a fancy updo to a neat ponytail.

She's. So. Freaking. Cute.

I have an overwhelming desire to wrap her up in a blanket and cuddle with her until we fall asleep together. I swallow slowly, reminding myself that one kiss doesn't give me the right to unlimited cuddles.

Molly sits on the bed, looking a little nervous and lacing her fingers together in front of her and then resting them on her outstretched legs. Her very smooth legs .... that now smell like french-lavender.

Facing her, I give her my full attention, waiting patiently for her to gather her thoughts and speak.

"Todd proposed to me today," she blurts suddenly.

My shoulders tense and I feel suddenly warmer in this onesie than I did a moment ago. "Excuse me?" I ask, thinking maybe I heard her wrong.

She hugs her knees to her chest. "Yeah. Apparently, our mothers arranged it and sprung it on me right before the wedding." Her head tilts to look at me. "I said no, obviously. But he told me something, and I can't stop thinking about it."

Breathing a sigh of relief that she turned him down, I unzip my onesie to my belly button. Because I'm starting to sweat. "What was it?"

Molly pulls her lips into her mouth, making me think back to our kiss earlier, then she looks down at her knees. "Well, for the past six years, I've received a plethora of gorgeous antique spoons." She finally looks at me again.

A bead of sweat drips down my back. Damn this onesie!

"They've all come with a note. Each one has been very sweet and romantic. Naturally, I thought it was Todd." She pauses but doesn't break eye contact. "But today he told me he has never sent me a spoon. Not once."

My throat feels thick and I clear my throat. "Really? How strange."

"The strangest thing is ... I just received one this morning. The prettiest one yet."

Wiping my sweaty brow on the sleeve of my onesie, I squeak out, "Yeah?"

"Yeah," she answers, a playful smile tugging at her lips. "My brain has been spinning all day, trying to think of who could be sending them. And unless my sister has been writing me love notes... my only other guess is... you."

The warm fabric of my onesie feels suffocating, sticking to my sweat and making my nervousness unbearable. My usual cool, confident persona is in shambles as the woman I've hidden my feelings for for years has found me out.

I stand from the bed and strip the onesie off—unable to tolerate it any longer—leaving me, once again, in nothing but boxer-briefs in front of my best friend. I pace next to the bed and drag a hand through my hair, trying to think of what to say.

Small, cool hands grip my arms gently. "It's okay, Brooks. I— I'm glad it was you."

I release a deep breath and look up to meet Molly's wide, blue eyes. The look on her face conveys vulnerability and a little apprehension. "Wait, what? Really?" Here I was worried she'd think I was a huge creep.

She huffs out a nervous laugh. "Yeah. Now I can keep them. I was about to donate them all, thinking Todd sent them."

My chest tightens, wondering what she means. Will she keep the spoons because she has feelings for me too? Or just because it wasn't Todd who sent them?

"But the notes," her expression grows serious. "Did you write those just to make me feel better? Or ... were the words real?"

Her eyes flit away from me, uncertainty clouding them. The tension in my body eases a little. Surely she wouldn't be asking me this if she didn't have *some* romantic feelings for me.

I bring my hands up to her cheeks and hold her face in my palms, making sure she can't look away from me. "Molly, I meant everything I wrote in those notes. Every single word."

My chin does a strange wobbly motion, and before I realize what's happening, moisture drips down my face.

I'm ... crying.

The built-up feelings from the last six years finally coming out feels like a weight lifting off of me. It's liberating.

"Oh, Brooks. I can't believe it took me this long to see how you felt. You've always been my biggest cheerleader and the person I went to for everything." Molly throws her arms around my waist and hugs me tightly.

Without delay, I hug her back. I can feel the rhythm of her breathing against my chest and it soothes something deep in my soul. Just the two of us, embracing and breathing in unison. The way we were always meant to be.

"These past few weeks, it's like someone removed my blindfold. I started to see how good we could be together." She pauses. "I have feelings for you too," she whispers against me, her breath tickling my skin.

"It was the underwear that did it, wasn't it?" I tease her, even though my heart is about to beat out of my chest and my stomach feels like I just rode the most intense roller coaster of my life. This woman I've wanted, but didn't dare to dream of a life with, *likes* me ... as more than just a friend.

Her laughter rumbles against my chest where her head is still resting against me. And for the first time, I allow myself to picture Molly in every aspect of my life: next to me at the weekly Windell family dinners, opening Christmas presents on Christmas morning, playing with my nieces and nephews, stealing secret kisses at the office.

Falling in love ... falling into bed at night. I can picture it all so clearly.

And it feels good.

Chapter 29

Molly

The warmth of Brooks's arms around me feels so nice after this long day, I don't pull away. His hand gently rubs my back in a soothing gesture, and I allow myself to lean into him, to carry all of my weight, to support me.

"How many spoons have you sent me over the years?"

"Thirteen," he answers quickly, not even having to think about it.

I hesitate for a moment before asking my next question, half terrified and half thrilled about what the answer could be. "Did you notice the initials on the one you gave me today?"

"Yes, I did ... M.W." He pulls back to look at me and his face is adorably flushed. "They're really nice initials, don't you think?" He smiles.

Now it's my turn to blush.

"You look exhausted, Molly. Let's get in bed?"

I nod and he walks over to my side of the bed and pulls down the covers. This gives me a good look at today's underwear. They're bubblegum pink and have squirrels on them holding acorns. The squirrels have little word bubbles so it looks like they're saying *I'm nuts about you*.

"Since I have thirteen gifts to make up for, I'm getting you new underwear."

He snickers and crawls over to his side of the bed. I slip into the blankets and we lay on our sides facing each other.

"Where do we go from here, Brooks?"

He smiles and reaches out to tuck a loose strand of hair behind my ear. "Well, I could possibly take you out on a *real* date ... instead of a fake one?"

"I think I'd like that." I smile. "Are you worried about the company, and us working together?"

"Nope," he answers confidently. "The great thing about being friends for so long is that we know each other's strengths and weaknesses. We know how to encourage each other, and how to solve conflict. Vanderwin Technologies has never gotten in the way of our friendship, so why would anything change when adding romance to the mix?"

His words give me peace. He's so confident in us. It reminds me of when he approached me in college with the idea of starting a company. He believed in us then, and he believes in us now. "That's very true. So, you don't think we'll get sick of each other?"

He snorts. "I could never get sick of you. You're my favorite human."

I smile sleepily, exhaustion making my eyelids feel heavy. I close them and whisper, "You're my favorite human too," before falling asleep.

The next morning, I wake up to the sound of the shower running. Surprised Brooks woke up before me, I check my phone on the nightstand.

I gasp when I see it's already five past ten. I never sleep this late, but I was so physically and emotionally exhausted from yesterday. I can't complain though; it ended wonderfully.

My dream last night wasn't of shirtless Vikings or pillaging ... but of Brooks as a dad, with a bunch of little blonde boys wrestling with him, his hair greying at the temples and adorable crow's feet at the corners of his eyes as he smiles.

It was even better than the Viking dream. Which is impressive, because the Viking dream was *really* good.

Brooks steps out of the bathroom. His hair is wet from the shower, but he's dressed for the day.

He grins at me. "Good morning, sleeping beauty."

I flop over and groan into my pillow. The bed dips down as I feel him sit on the edge of the bed by my legs.

"We kind of need to figure out how today is going to go," he says, his voice sounding hesitant. "I don't fly out until this afternoon, and I'm pretty sure your mother still hates my guts."

Rolling over, I prop myself up against the headboard. "Yeah, it's going to be a little awkward. And I'm not supposed to leave until the day after Christmas. Maybe we can move our flights up?"

His mouth pulls up in a half smile. "I'm not trying to move too fast, or freak you out ... but I'm gonna be upfront with you, okay?" He raises an eyebrow in question.

"Okay ..." I say with hesitation.

"I don't just want to date you, Molly. I want to *pursue* you. I want to be with you. I know it will take time for you to see how serious I am, since I have a reputation for dating a different person every week." He inhales a deep breath and breathes it out slowly. "But I'll spend every waking moment showing you that you're the only one for me."

A grin slowly spreads across my face. He's been showing me for the past six years how he feels about me. If that's not playing the long game, I don't know what is. "I believe you. Your dating history is in the past, as is mine."

He sighs in relief. "But being with you means also being with your family. It's a package deal. So, I think we should rip off the band-aid instead of fleeing for our lives."

My smile droops and I stare at him for a moment, trying to wrap my mind around this new (to me) version of my best friend. This serious, passionate version. Finally, I nod in agreement. "You're right. We're going to have several hurdles to get past for this to work. One being owning a company together ... the other being my family. So we'll get one of them out of the way today, then?"

He chuckles. "Well, Rome wasn't built in a day. But I'll never earn their respect or approval by running away like a scaredy-cat."

"But what if *I* want to run away like a scaredy-cat?" I stick my bottom lip out, making him laugh.

"You can fly home. But I'm not leaving until your parents adore me." He winks.

"Well, it's been nice knowing you. I guess I'll never see you again."

He lunges forward and starts tickling my sides. Brooks is touching me, and he smells *really* good. I wish we could stay locked up in this room, basking in our happiness for a while. But, alas, my parents.

His tickling comes to a stop, and he grows serious, almost self-conscious—which is a new expression for him. "You really don't think they'll ever come around?" he asks, looking genuinely bummed.

I place my hand on top of his, rubbing my thumb against his skin in an attempt to ease his worries. "It's impossible not to like you, Brooks. But it's definitely going to take some time."

"You're right," he concedes. "Well, get dressed muffin butt. Let's do this."

I roll my eyes at the pet name, but get out of bed and head toward the closet. I don't move fast enough though, and he smacks my butt as I walk by him.

Half an hour later, Brooks and I walk into the living room. The perk of sleeping in today is that everyone else has already departed. I'm sure Preston and Mildred are halfway to their honeymoon in Bali by now. I'm not worried about them anyway; I'm pretty sure they're both team Brooks after the past few days.

The house is put back in order already. You can't even tell there had been an extravagant wedding that took place here just last night. My parents are sitting in the armchairs in front of the fireplace, my mother reading a book, and my father working on his laptop.

Their heads tilt upwards as we walk in. They stare at us without speaking.

"Good morning," I say, breaking the silence.

My father looks at his wristwatch. "Barely," he mutters.

My mother looks back down at her book.

"Listen," Brooks says, moving forward with confidence. "I want us to be on good terms. I intend to spend a lot of time with your daughter, which means you're going to have to tolerate me. Eventually. So, let's get everything out in the open." He sits down in the armchair nearest to my father, resting his forearms on his knees. "Why do you think Todd is better for your daughter than me?"

My eyes widen; I wasn't expecting him to go there. My mother gasps, and my father slides his glasses down his nose.

"This conversation is entirely inappropriate," my mother says indignantly.

"Here are the reasons I'm better for Molly." Brooks holds up a hand and ticks off his list with his fingers. "(1) I respect her, (2) We already know we work well together, (3) I love antiquing, (4) She's always cold and I'm always hot ... match made in heaven, (5) —"

My father holds up a hand to silence him. "Okay, we get the picture."

My mother stands to her feet, her angry eyes not leaving Brooks's face. "Listen here, young man. You're not a parent, therefore you don't understand what it's like to hope and dream for your child's future." She pauses, her eyes softening slightly. "You have to realize me and my best friend had babies within days of each other. One a boy ... one a girl." She smiles in my direction. "Of course, we always wanted them to end up together and strengthen our bond even more."

Brooks looks at my mother with a hint of sympathy, but the tense set of his shoulders tells me he's still irritated. "You're right. I don't understand what it's like to have a child. But when I do have children, someday, I like to think I'd want them to be happy ... and to be with someone who takes care of them. Someone who loves them unconditionally."

I study Brooks, his words sending a shiver through me. We've solidified the fact that he's had feelings for me, but love? Does he *love* me?

My mother sits back down, crossing her legs at her ankles and studying her hands. "I really think Todd just needs more time to mature."

My newfound gumption for standing up for myself lights a fire inside my soul. I step forward and look directly at my mother. "I refuse to be a pawn in your plans any longer, Mother. Todd doesn't even begin to deserve my affection. And if you can't see that … that's on you. Not me."

My mother brings her bejeweled fingers to her chest with a shocked inhale of breath. I've always tolerated her criticism and penchant for having the last word. But not today, and not when it comes to who I'm with.

My father blinks slowly a few times, possibly still grasping the way I just spoke to my mother. Finally, he turns his attention to his wife. "I'm sorry, darling, but I have to agree with Molly here. Todd is a lost cause."

My mother sends him a harsh look. "He's only twenty-six!" She defends.

He heaves an exasperated sigh. "When I was that age, I had already taken over my father's insurance company. And look at Brooks and Molly." He gestures between us with one hand. "Both the same age as Todd and running a successful company together."

I smile at my father, appreciating his support. He gives me a proud, fatherly smile back, and nods his head slightly, as if praising me for speaking my mind for once.

Brooks's hand slides into mine and he gives my hand a gentle squeeze.

"Brooks, I don't know you well enough to give you my blessing, or whatever it is you're looking for. But please just keep that pipsqueak, Todd, away from my daughter." My father ignores my mother's gasp of horror and goes back to working on his computer.

"It would be my pleasure, sir," Brooks says with a sly grin and a nod of his head.

My mother begins lecturing my father and we make a quick escape from the room.

"Want to grab some lunch?" Brooks asks, pulling me toward the front door.

"Sounds perfect."

Chapter 30

Brooks

That afternoon, I'm on my flight with Molly by my side. She moved hers up, deciding she'd had enough of her mother's dramatics for one week. Once we're in the air, Molly turns toward me, a look of determination on her face. "I think we should keep our relationship on the down low until your dating ban is over."

My eyebrows raise. "I'm pretty sure my dating ban is over." I raise our joined hands to prove my point.

"I know that, and you know that. But if your brother finds out ..."

"The naked walk of shame at my mother's garden party," I say in my spookiest voice. I'm being playful, but on the inside, I'm absolutely dreading the humiliation. Plus, can't you get arrested for stuff like that?

She wrinkles her nose. "Honestly? I don't want anyone seeing you naked ... I don't care if they're sixty. And it's only like three more weeks.

"Whoa, you're hot when you're territorial."

She slaps my arm and I laugh. "If you want to keep things quiet for three more weeks, I'm on board. I mean, I don't want my mother's country club friends lusting after me."

Molly rolls her eyes.

The flight attendant stops at our row and takes our drink orders. Before she leaves she looks at me and does a double take. "Oh my gosh! Brooks?" her eyelashes flutter and she leans an arm on the seat in front of me.

She looks faintly familiar, but I can't quite place her. I smile politely. "Hey, great to see you," I say, pretending to remember her.

Her expression tells me she doesn't buy it. "You took me on a date last year, and we had a great time. And then you never returned my calls."

"Right." I grimace, finally remembering her. "Sorry about that. I got busy. Life, you know." I laugh awkwardly and shrug.

She looks at me, unamused, then turns to Molly. Molly is watching our interaction like it's the best entertainment she's had in months.

"I can see you've been *very* busy," the flight attendant deadpans. "Anyway, I'll be back soon with your drinks." There's an evil twinkle in her eyes, and I decide then that it's probably best not to drink whatever she brings me.

Molly snickers next to me once the woman is out of earshot.

"Not funny," I grit out with a tight smile.

"Does that happen often?" she asks, looking curious but not offended. I grimace in lieu of a response.

Molly just sighs. "I suppose I'm going to have to learn to deal with that."

Smiling, I lean in and kiss her. "I only have eyes for you."

"I know. And you've had to deal with Todd all these years, so I can handle it. I think." She bumps her shoulder into mine.

After her experience with Todd, I can't imagine it will always be this easy when she's reminded of my past. I need to make sure to show her constantly that she means more to me than anyone in the world. That all of those dates were wasted, a means of trying to forget her. To ease the pain of seeing her with another guy. But it was all futile.

She leans her head on my shoulder and I enjoy the feel of having her there.

"Oh, hey. What about Christmas?" I ask, remembering that today is Christmas Eve.

"What about it?" she says in a half yawn, like she was about to fall asleep.

"It's tomorrow. And I want you to spend it with me." I hesitate. "But my family would speculate."

Her head pops up and I can see by her bright eyes that her brain is working on a master plan. "How about I stop by to have you sign a contract or something? Diane will inevitably invite me to stay."

"You and my mom are on a first-name basis already?"

She ignores me and continues with her idea. "I'll even bring some wine and cookies, and say I was heading to a party I wasn't really that excited about."

"Brilliant! They definitely won't see through that!"

Molly shoves me playfully. I love all of her little touches, even this.

"Do you have any better ideas?"

I scratch my chin while I think. "How about this? When I get to my parents' house on Christmas day, I'll tell my mom you're going to be alone this Christmas. Naturally, she'll be horrified. Then I'll ask if she can save a plate of food for me to take to you." I give Molly a smug look, knowing my idea is way better. "My mother will not only demand that I go get you immediately, but will also lecture me for being a horrible person and not bringing you with me in the first place."

Her eyebrows raise, clearly impressed.

After landing back home in Kansas, I can tell Molly is tired. The past few weeks have been an emotional whirlwind for her. As much as I want to continue spending time with her, I know she needs some rest.

Parking in her driveway, I grab her suitcase and carry it for her. She rushes ahead of me to unlock the door, holding it open for me. I kiss her cheek as I shuffle past her. She giggles and closes the door behind us.

I roll the suitcase to a stop in the entryway and turn toward her. "I'm going to head out and let you have some peace and quiet," I say, taking a step toward her front door.

A brief look of disappointment passes her features before she forces a smile. "Oh, okay."

Taking a step toward her, I pull her into my arms. "You know I'd rather hang out with you than anything else in the world." I lean back so I can look at her. "But you're about to faint with exhaustion. You need sleep."

She groans and snuggles against me. "You're right. I can't wait to see you tomorrow. It's actually going to be a little weird not sleeping next to you." Her body tenses and she pulls away. "I'm sorry. That was too clingy, wasn't it?"

I chuckle before I can stop myself. "You're *not* the clingy one. I'm the one who was secretly sending you spoons and love notes for six years, remember?"

Laughing, her body relaxes. "Okay, true."

"Don't ever hide what you're thinking or feeling from me, okay? I can handle it all." I hug her once more and drop a kiss on top of her head. "Goodnight, Molly. I *will* see you tomorrow."

"Can't wait."

―――*ell*―――

The next day, I stride inside my parents' house as planned. David is the first one I see, and I run up behind him and wrap my arms around him. "Big brother! I've missed you!"

David shoves me away, but there's a subtle smirk on his face. "Hey. It's nice to be back in the States for a bit."

It's still weird to me that my serious, al-ways-has-a-plan brother changed his whole life around when he fell in love with his wife, Isa. He would've been the last person I'd have thought would elope and move out of the country. A testament to how much he loves his wife.

"You look good. Marriage suits you," I say honestly, then stick my hand in my pockets awkwardly since we aren't usually this complimentary with each other. But hell, I really have missed him.

"Thanks, man." He smiles and Isa appears from the kitchen.

She comes to stand next to him and loops an arm around his waist. "Hey, Brooks! So, how's the dating ban going?" Her eyes twinkle mischievously like she knows something I don't.

"Great. It's been a nice break, actually," I answer with all the confidence I can muster. Trying not to think about Molly or I'll give myself away.

"Oh, good. Glad to hear it." She winks and kisses David's cheek before running off to the kitchen again.

David stares at me with a smirk.

"What?"

He raises his eyebrows and shakes his head innocently. "Nothing. Let's go help Mom with dinner."

I follow him inside the bustling kitchen, where the rest of the family is doing my mother's bidding. Drew and Sophie are on mashed potato duty, Madden and Odette are getting the pies ready to bake in the oven, and David begins helping Isa form dough into rolls. My father is likely in the backyard smoking the turkey, and Mom is frantically fussing over everything, and nothing in particular.

"Oh, Brooks! Thank goodness. I need someone to set the table." She grabs a stack of plates and thrusts them into my hands.

I lean over and give her a quick kiss on the cheek. "Nice to see you too, Mom."

She stops what she's doing and palms my cheek affectionately, before patting it a bit too aggressively. I wince. "Okay, now get to work."

I turn toward the dining room before remembering my plan. "Oh, hey."

Mom turns toward me again, wiping her hands on her apron. "Yes?"

"Molly had originally planned to stay in Vermont for Christmas, but her sister's wedding really wore her out. She flew home early, and now she'll be home alone all day." My mother looks at me impatiently, waiting for me to make my point. "I didn't know if we could save her a plate of food, and I'll take it to her on my way home?"

The kitchen quiets down abruptly, and all of my siblings and their spouses turn to stare at me. Madden shakes his head in dismay and Odette pinches his arm in warning. Drew and Sophie look at each other, grinning. And David and Isa have the same mischievous smirks on their faces that I saw earlier.

What the heck is going on?

My mom smiles and seems remarkably unperturbed that I left Molly alone on Christmas. "Sweetheart, just go get her after you're done setting the table, all right?"

My brows furrow in confusion and I nod. "Oh, okay. Are you sure that's all right?"

"Of course. I already have presents for her," Mom says with a smile, then turns and continues cleaning up the kitchen.

Confused, I walk into the dining room and set the table.

Then I drive over and get Molly.

Chapter 31

Molly

When we arrive at Brooks's parents' house, I'm feeling nervous. On the drive over, he told me they were acting weird. What if they've already found us out somehow?

We walk inside without knocking, something I think is very endearing about the Windells; their door is always open to their kids.

His parents meet us in the front entryway. "Merry Christmas, Molly!"

I hand her a box of maple candies I brought from Vermont. "Sorry, it's not much."

"Nonsense, this is lovely!" She takes the candies from me politely.

"Glad you could make it, Molly," Mr. Windell says in his serious tone.

I study him for a few seconds, noting his blonde hair that's half grey now, and his tall, slender build with the same broad shoulders Brooks has. I imagine he's in his sixties but is still very handsome. I can't help but wonder if this is a replica of what Brooks might look like in about forty years.

"Thank you for having me ... again," I tease, and they laugh politely.

Mr. Windell guides us into the dining room. It's decked out with holiday decor and the table is set beautifully. Each place setting has a calligraphy place card, and there's one with my name on it ... right between Madden and David.

Brooks's eyes shift around the table, and his eyes widen when he sees we're not seated together. Instead, he's seated on the other side of the table, next to Drew and Sophie.

He attempts to act unbothered as he takes his seat and I take mine.

Madden grins at me, and says, "You have the best seat in the house."

"I was about to say the same thing," David agrees.

They each take a sip from their water glasses, trying to hide their smirks.

I laugh, and sneak a glance at Brooks, whose knuckles are white as he grips his fork tightly. This isn't good. They totally *know*. But how?

The thought of Brooks traipsing nude in front of a bunch of older ladies makes my stomach twist. What if one of them has a heart attack?

Mr. Windell quickly says grace, then everyone digs into their food, eating their fill. Laughter and chatter fill the room, along with giggles from the children. This is so much more fun than Christmas with my family. *And* they actually eat.

"So, Brooks, how was your business trip?" David asks before taking a bite of potatoes.

Brooks narrows his eyes slightly as he chews his food. He swallows and answers, "It was lovely. So much snow."

The two brothers continue looking at each other, both unblinking, obviously in some kind of staring contest.

"What's the vegetation like there?" Sophie says, drawing them back to the present.

Brooks looks at her, clearly confused. "The vegetation?"

"Yeah," Drew says. "We've heard there's a lot of mistletoe in Vermont."

Brooks rolls his lips together. "Hm. I haven't heard that."

David grunts. "Odd. Even I knew Vermont was famous for their mistletoe."

Brooks smiles tightly. I attempt to smooth things over. "They're actually known for their maple syrup, I believe."

The siblings look at me with amused expressions.

"How was your sister's wedding, Molly?" Sophie asks. "Weren't you planning to stay through Christmas? Not that we aren't thrilled to have you with us!" She adds with a bright smile.

"The wedding was great! It was just ... stressful. And I was ready to get home."

Sophie nods. "That makes sense."

Madden and Odette's boys run to their parents, both jumping up and down in anticipation. "Can we open presents now?"

"Not until we're done eating," Odette says calmly, then sends them back to their seats.

They pout before walking away but cheer up when their grandpa sneaks them candy as they pass by him. I smile at the scene. The Windells are wealthy and successful, but they're not stuffy and formal. Although I think that fact mildly annoys Diane.

I can picture coming here with Brooks each year, hanging out with his siblings, and maybe someday ... in the *very* distant future ... having our own children running around and sneaking candy.

Once we're finished eating, we're quickly ushered into the living room by the children. Brooks finds me and places his hand on my back before leaning in and whispering, "Do you think they know?"

"Oh, they definitely know," I whisper back. "They're trying to fake us out, make us admit we're together."

"Stay strong. Don't give in," he says, pinning me with a serious look.

I nod and give him a mock salute, making him chuckle. We sit on the floor beside each other and watch the kids pass out gifts. I'm surprised to see I have a pile of presents just like everyone else does. I look at Brooks, my eyebrows raised in question, and he just shrugs his shoulders.

The children open their gifts first, ripping into them with pure joy. The boys bring their toys to Brooks and ask him to put them together. He happily agrees, being a giant kid himself.

Mrs. Windell claps her hands together. "All right, now time for the adults! This year, we're going to start with the oldest and then end with the youngest."

Brooks's mouth falls open for a moment. "But we've *always* done the youngest first."

Madden quickly sticks his tongue out at Brooks before Diane can see him and rips into one of his presents. Odette yanks it away from him, a teasing smile on her face. "Excuse me, *I'm* the oldest."

Madden groans and mutters, "Barely."

Once it's finally Brooks's turn, he rips into his pile with as much gumption as the children did. David rolls his eyes at the scene.

When he opens the second to last one, he stops and stares at the contents of the box. David, Madden, and Drew give each other knowing smirks.

Everyone seems to know what's inside the box, except me. I try looking over Brooks's shoulder, but he's so tall. Finally, he angles the box for me to see.

There's nothing inside except a recent gossip magazine. I'm confused at first until I spot the name of one of the articles inside: *Du Pont Media's billionaire heir gets hitched.*

Without delay, I grab the magazine and turn to the article. I read it out loud, "Preston Du Pont, heir to half of the multi-billion dollar company, Du Pont Media, married Mildred Annelise Vanderbilt this week in a lavish ceremony at her family's Vermont mansion."

I scan the pictures in the article and gasp when I come to a large one of me and Brooks kissing under the mistletoe awning. I read the caption aloud, "Are wedding bells in the air for Mildred's younger sister Mary Elizabeth too?"

David rubs his hands together conspiratorially. "I guess we'll be coming back to the States sooner rather than later," he says to Isa.

She beams at him, clearly enjoying the drama. "Perhaps ... in the spring?"

Mrs. Windell, who obviously doesn't know the terms of the bet, looks pleased. "Oh, how wonderful! You're both welcome to come home as often as you'd like!"

Drew grins. "You want to increase our workouts? I'm sure you want to look good."

"Why are you guys being weird?" Diane asks, looking around the room. "I for one am thrilled that Brooks is dating Molly."

"It's about time," Mr. Windell says dryly.

Brooks runs a hand through his hair and heaves a resigned sigh. "Well, at least we don't have to keep this a secret anymore?"

"The silver lining?" I smile up at him.

Madden clears his throat loudly. "I believe you have one more present to open."

Brooks eyes the small present warily, then picks it up. He shakes it a few times, then opens it tentatively, like something's going to jump out at him.

When the box is finally open, he laughs and pulls out a branch of mistletoe. Holding it above us with one hand, he gives me that irresistible smolder that I remember from the hot tub in Vermont.

I bring my hands up to his face, cupping his cheeks in my palms. I smile before pulling his face down closer to mine. Brooks's free hand lands on my waist and pulls me closer to him, his fingertips grazing the sliver of skin that's exposed just above my jeans. I close the distance between us, unable to resist his lips any longer. He stills, letting me lead, but his lips are soft and pliant against mine. I kiss him leisurely; I'm in no hurry.

The adults whistle and clap, but the kids make gagging noises. I can feel Brooks smiling against my lips. When we pull apart and I look into his eyes, I have an overwhelming feeling of contentment ... despite knowing a bunch of older women will see my boyfriend nude in a few months.

Chapter 32

Brooks

I'm heading into work early the next morning, feeling like a mean boss opening the office up the day after Christmas ... but in my defense, everyone was off the entire time Molly and I were in Vermont. Except for the few times Hope went in to check messages, but I gave her a nice Christmas bonus, so I think she'll be okay.

Yesterday was incredible, and I'm still on a high from it. I've always loved Christmas. The presents, the food, the music. What's not to love?

But having Molly there with me made it even better. Watching her interact with my family, playing with my nieces and nephews, and sitting next to her while we opened presents. It was everything I'd never allowed myself to dream of. Everything I didn't think I'd ever get to experience.

I can't manage to wipe the smile off my face as I walk inside the office. Hope is sitting at the front desk, as usual. But today, she's grinning like a fool and eyeing me with a knowing look.

"Good morning, Hope," I say, patting the top of her desk with my hand.

"Oh, I *bet* it is, Mr. Windell. You're bright-eyed and bushy-tailed this morning! Any reason for that?" She rests her elbows on the desk, smiling up at me with a mischievous grin.

I pretend not to know what she's referring to. Molly told me Hope and Layla saw the article and were blowing up her phone with texts yesterday. "I just had a really great Christmas," I answer with a smile.

She hums and swivels in her chair to grab something out of the printer.

Knowing I have to walk by Layla's desk as well before reaching Molly, I brace myself for her commentary.

Sure enough, Layla makes a show of looking at her watch. "Wow. So early. Any particular reason you were in such a hurry to get to work today?"

I lean against her desk and feign ignorance. "I just missed you all so much. Five days is way too long."

"You're a terrible actor." She chuckles.

Smiling, I shrug away from her desk and walk toward Molly's office. I can see her through the glass walls, sitting in her large, leather office chair. Looking impossibly beautiful.

I let myself into her office, and her head tilts up. When she sees me, she grins and stands from her seat. She reaches for me without realizing what she's doing, and I don't want to stop her. But she insisted yesterday that we keep things strictly professional at work.

I glance at her outstretched arms and quirk a brow. She grimaces before grabbing one of my hands and shaking it awkwardly.

"Good morning, coworker," she says formally, then bursts into laughter.

Using our joined hands, I pull her closer to me, close enough that I could lean down and kiss her if she'd let me. "Good morning, muffin butt."

"Are you ever going to stop calling me that?" she pulls her hand out of mine but doesn't step away.

"It's kind of stuck now." I shrug.

She crosses her arms, looking annoyed and amused at the same time. "Why are you here so early, by the way?"

Taking a tiny step forward, I bring our faces even closer together. "For some reason, I was really excited to get to work today."

Her tongue peeks out, wetting her bottom lip and I nearly groan with the unbearable desire to kiss her.

"You guys realize the walls are glass, right?" Layla's voice rings through the office.

We look over and find the entire office staring at us, watching our interaction, and looking extremely amused. I clear my throat and Molly takes a step away from me, a deep blush coloring her cheeks.

"Sorry," I whisper.

"Keeping things professional is going to be harder than I thought," she admits with a sheepish smile.

"Yeah." I chuckle. "Oh, hey. I have an idea I want to talk to you about when you have time."

She narrows her eyes and sits back down in her office chair. "Is this a trick? Are you trying to lure me away and make out with me in a closet or something?"

"No. But I'm really mad I hadn't thought of that."

She snickers and opens her laptop. "I'm going to be tied down all morning with catch-up work. Can we talk about it at lunch?"

"Perfect, it's a date." I wink, drawing a smile from her. I'll never tire of seeing her smile at me like this.

"So, what did you want to talk about?" Molly asks before taking a bite of her sandwich.

We're having lunch at our favorite cafe, and it feels good to be here for the first time as a real couple. Last time we were here, Todd showed up with Trudy and I was pretending to be romantically involved with Molly. But now? I really am. I grin, unable to help myself, and Molly eyes me curiously from across the table.

I steeple my hands in front of me and look at her. "Well, I was thinking. You're always the one who puts your own desires aside to make things easier for everyone else. But I don't want you to do that with me. Not at work, and not in our relationship. I want you to tell me what you're thinking, I want you to disagree with me when you want to, and I want you to be completely honest with me."

She nods hesitantly, and I continue, "Your degree is the same as mine. And in college, you were amazing with design. I would never have completed our original implant design without you."

"Okay," she says, looking a little confused.

"If you miss the biomedical engineering side of things, you need to tell me. I never meant to take over the lab. It's *our* company. We can always hire a business manager, if that's what you want."

Her eyes fill with unshed tears, I unclasp my hands and reach for hers. She sniffs. "Sorry, it's just ... I'm not used to anyone wanting my opinion or encouraging me to voice them. It means so much to me that you do that."

I rub my thumbs along the back of her hands in a circular pattern, hoping to comfort her with my touch. She blinks back her tears and smiles. "I really do enjoy the business side of things. But I can't lie: I miss being in the lab and working on a project."

Blowing out a sigh of relief, I chuckle. "Okay, whew. Because this knee replacement design is killing me. And I don't think I can do it without you."

She laughs. "I'm pretty sure you could, but the idea of helping with it makes me excited." Molly pauses, looking thoughtful. "This may sound demanding ... but can I do both? Can we hire a part-time manager?"

I scoff. "Molly, you're the least demanding person I know. And yes, I'm sure we can find a part-time manager. We'll start looking, or we can even hire from within?"

She beams at me. "Okay. I'm excited!"

"Me too." I wink. "Although, I'm not sure I'll get any work done when you're in the lab right next to me."

She shakes her head disapprovingly, but I see the smile she's trying to hide. "Hurry up and eat, Mr. Windell. We have work to do."

I raise an eyebrow. "You're a mean boss."

The sound of a throat clearing draws us out of our happy little bubble and we look up. Hope and Layla are standing in front of our table. Hope looks between us, and she's nervously playing with her fingers. Layla is looking down at the floor like it's the most interesting thing in the world. They look ... guilty.

"We thought you two would be here," Hope says.

Layla takes a deep breath. "We kind of have something to get off our chests."

Molly looks surprised, and maybe a little worried. "Okay, what is it?"

Layla and Hope look at each other briefly before Layla speaks again, "That note you found on Todd's car?"

Hope quickly adds, "We wrote that."

Molly's eyebrows raise slightly. "What? Really?"

"It's just ... we knew Todd was seeing her behind your back because Layla was also getting her hair done by Trudy," Hope speaks nervously, her voice a little too loud and her hands flying around as she speaks.

Layla motions for her to calm down. "I don't go to her anymore!" Layla insists, her expression so serious, I have a hard time not laughing.

"We were just trying to help." Hope's eyes look sad and apologetic. "But we see how much stress it caused you, and also the drama with your sister's wedding."

"But we're glad everything worked out." Layla gestures between me and Molly.

Molly looks reflective and doesn't say anything for what feels like several minutes. It's probably only ten seconds, but we're all waiting anxiously to see how she'll respond.

Finally, she laughs. "Which one of you kissed the note?"

Hope raises her hand, and Molly starts laughing harder. Hope and Layla smile, both looking apprehensive about her outburst.

Amused, I grin at Molly, who's still laughing.

Dabbing at the corners of her eyes with a napkin, her laughter begins to slow. "I mean, I guess I should thank you both. It finally convinced me to end things with Todd. Indefinitely," Molly says, smiling genuinely at her friends.

Molly stands and pulls them both into a big hug. "But for real. No more meddling. Okay?"

"We promise!" Hope says, her voice muffled since her face is in Molly's hair.

"And we're so sorry!" Layla adds, wrapping her arms tightly around Hope and Molly.

The three women end their embrace and they turn and look at me, as if just now remembering I'm still here. Their expressions turn expectant, like they're waiting for me to finally say something.

I stand from my seat, Hope and Layla eyeing me hesitantly. I grin, and they relax. Then I shake their hands with all the enthusiasm I feel. "You both are the true heroes of Christmas. Thank you."

We burst into laughter, drawing the attention of everyone else in the restaurant. I take one giant step toward Molly, my girl. She smiles up at me, her eyes reflecting the same happiness I feel.

I take her beautiful face in my hands and kiss her the way I've wanted to all damn day. She melts into me, wrapping her arms around my neck. I ignore the chuckles and whispers from the other restaurant patrons, not caring who sees us.

Molly

Three Months Later

A thorn from the bush I'm hiding in pokes me in the side. "Ouch," I whisper.

David glares at me. "Shh!"

I mouth the word *sorry*, and he calms down. Isa gives me a sympathetic smile, as if to apologize for her husband taking this all so seriously.

Madden and Odette are hidden in a bush nearby, watching the garden party closely via binoculars. They're both grinning, clearly enjoying this way too much.

Sophie is standing a few yards away near the gate that leads into the garden at the country club. She has a walkie-talkie in hand, as does Drew, who's hidden behind a tree right in front of the bushes. I stifle a laugh because that tree doesn't stand a chance of concealing Drew's large form. Sophie calls him Mr. Muscles for a reason.

We have a clear view of the entire garden and one of the country club's elaborate water fountains. This one reminds me of the large fountain the characters from *Friends* play in during the opening theme song.

The garden party is on the patio near the fountain. The long table is filled with extravagant floral arrangements and lace tablecloths. All the women are dressed up and wearing ostentatious hats like they're British or something.

An announcement comes through the overhead speakers, "Mrs. Windell, you're needed at the front desk. Please come as soon as you're able."

"Oh dear." I can hear Diane's voice faintly, and she stands from her seat. The other women fuss at her to ignore it and sit back down. But much to our relief, she walks through the garden gate and toward the front entrance of the country club. We listen with bated breath until the sound of her heels clacking on the pavement fades completely.

Sophie starts talking into her walkie-talkie, and I can hear what she's saying through Drew's end. "Mama bird has left the old hens. I repeat: Mama bird has left the old hens."

Drew looks back at the rest of us and we grin at him. He pushes the button on his walkie-talkie and speaks in a hushed voice, "All clear. Release the baby bird."

Sophie smirks, looking toward the garden entrance on the opposite side of the country club. She waves and then *caws* loudly several times, like an eagle. We all snicker from where we're still hiding in the bushes.

Brooks glides confidently through the gate and winks at our hiding place, even adding finger guns. He's wearing nothing but a red speedo.

Yes, I convinced his siblings to change the terms of the bet. They didn't put up much of a fight, since deep down they knew the nudity idea was bound to get Brooks arrested.

Brooks's body is oiled up and ready for his fountain swim. His abs glisten in the sunlight and draw my attention to that glorious V shape that disappears beneath the speedo. As he draws nearer to the garden party, the women gasp in offense ... but they don't look away.

He grins at them and waves before leisurely sinking into the water fountain. He allows the water to spray his hair and he shakes it out dramatically. I snicker at the show he's giving these ladies.

Thank goodness Drew is a doctor. Some of them may need CPR after this.

It only takes a minute for the ladies to relax. They begin giggling and grinning at each other. One of them even throws a few dollar bills in Brooks's direction. He captures them in his hand and blows her a kiss.

When we hear the clacking of Diane's heels on the pavement again, I clear my throat three times ... the signal. Drew glances back at me and nods once, pressing the button on his walkie-talkie once more. "Mama bird is heading back to the nest. This is not a drill."

Sophie clears her throat three times, getting Brooks's attention, then rolls her head from one shoulder to the next. Brooks knows that's his cue to get the heck out of there. He blows some more kisses to his new fans, and walks quickly toward the other gate, making a clean escape.

We're all so focused on Brooks, we don't notice Diane walking toward the bushes. "What are you all doing here?" she asks, her arms crossed and her high-heeled foot tapping on the grass.

David tries to duck down lower. "I already saw you, David!"

Sophie grimaces when she sees her mother's annoyed stance and quietly tip-toes backward toward the same gate Brooks escaped through. Diane swivels her head. "I already saw you, too!"

Sophie stops abruptly and pouts. She stalks toward our group, giving up any hope of escaping.

"Now. I want an explanation." She narrows her eyes on Madden and Odette. "And why do you two have that ridiculous camouflage paint all over your faces?"

Madden gulps, his Adam's apple bobbing nervously. "We just … wanted to see what a garden party was like."

"Yeah," David nods enthusiastically. Er, as enthusiastic as David can be, anyway. "We've never been invited. And we were just … fascinated."

"It was my fault," Isa comes to his defense. "I've never seen a country club before!"

Diane looks at her children with obvious suspicion and disappointment. Drew makes the mistake of shuffling his feet, and a branch cracks beneath his foot. She looks back and sees him for the first time, gasping in shock.

"You too, Drew? You're the sweet one!"

He looks down at his feet. "I'm sorry, Diane."

Diane shakes her head and sets her fists on her hips. "I have to get back to the party … but I *will* get to the bottom of this. And you all better not have done anything that could embarrass me … or the Windell reputation."

Isa snorts, trying unsuccessfully to suppress a laugh. She's promptly met with the steely gaze of each Windell sibling.

After giving us all one final glare, Diane strides back to her garden party.

—*ele*—

We left the country club faster than a getaway driver leaving a bank robbery, none of us wanting to endure any more questions from Diane Windell. We decided to meet back at Madden and Odette's penthouse for lunch. Brooks is dressed now, wearing some distressed jeans, a red cotton tee, and, of course, a backward baseball cap.

Once we're alone in the elevator at Madden's building, Brooks reaches for me. He still smells like tanning oil and his arms are a little greasy. "Did you enjoy the show?" He winks.

"Not as much as the old lady who threw money at you."

He throws his head back and laughs, then reaches into his back pocket, pulling out the cash the woman gave him. "It's all yours, just like everything else I have to give," he says sweetly as he tucks the money into my jeans pocket.

I smile and wrap my arms around his waist. His hands quickly move to my back and pull my body against his. "You're so warm," he says, sneaking his ice-cold hands up the back of my shirt. "That water was freezing."

Giggling, I try to squirm away from him. "You're always hot, so soak it up while you can!"

Brooks's strong embrace is impossible to get out of. Not that I really want to anyway. He relents, removing his hands from my skin and sticking them inside the back pockets of my jeans instead.

Standing on my toes, I give him a quick kiss.

"You're not getting away with that lousy little peck. I've just been through hell. Comfort me, woman!" He wraps his arms around me and lifts me off the ground. He sighs happily before brushing his lips against mine. He kisses me so gently, and so softly before changing the angle and deepening the kiss. The way he kisses me makes me lose sense of all time and all space. I get lost in it.

I wrap my legs around his waist, trying to get closer to him. Brooks smiles against my lips at my eagerness, then rests my back against the wall of the elevator. He continues to kiss me like I've never been kissed before. I just saw him at work yesterday, and yet, I can't seem to get enough of him.

He pulls back and rests his forehead against mine. "I love you, Muffin Butt."

"I love you too, Hunky Bear."

"Are you guys ready for lunch yet?" Madden's voice surprises us, and we notice that the elevator door has opened.

All of Brooks's siblings and their spouses are staring at us with their arms crossed, humor dancing in their eyes.

Brooks slowly releases me and I stand next to him, my cheeks flaming. He takes my hand and leads me out of the elevator.

"Heck yes. I'm starving! Being eye candy for a bunch of old ladies is exhausting."

His siblings roll their eyes and head inside the penthouse. Brooks winks at me before pulling me inside with him.

I've never felt so seen, so loved, and so content. Because here I am, with my very best friend in the world. My biggest fan, the one who's always supported me. The one who knows all my faults, and doesn't care about my past ... And, in turn, I don't care about his either.

Because he's my future, and I'm his.

And that's all that matters.

Bonus Epilogue

Can't say goodbye to the Windells yet? Use the QR code below to subscribe to my newsletter and you'll receive a free bonus epilogue!

(This is an epic glimpse of the family twenty years in the future and you don't want to miss it).

Also By

Under Kansas Skies Series:

Running Mate (Madden & Odette)

House Mate (Sophie & Drew)

Check Mate (David & Isabella)

Cabin Mate (Brooks & Molly)

Hooked on a Feeling Hockey Series:

Passion or Penalty (Free prequel novella)!

Desire or Defense (Pre-order)

Acknowledgments

Thank you a million (actually, a billion) times to my BETA readers, Amanda, Madi, and Katie! You guys gave me the BEST input and I love you for it. Also, thank you to my editor, Amy Guan for polishing Cabin Mate up and making her shine!

And thank you to all my Bookstagram friends. Your excitement over this book kept me typing away!

I hope with all my heart that you adore Brooks' story, and that you enjoyed hanging out with the Windells as much as I did. I'm sure going to miss them.

About Author

Leah writes romantic comedies sure to make you laugh out loud and swoon at the same time. Although she's a Kansas girl at heart, Leah is a proud Air Force spouse and currently lives in Ohio with her husband, three children, and Maine Coon cat.

Made in the USA
Monee, IL
09 December 2023

48626581R00194